A DESPERATE RACE

All at once the hairs at the back of Kit's neck began to tingle and rise. Although he never understood why it happened, he knew that when it did it was time to dive for cover!

Kit swiveled about in his saddle. About a mile off, a string of Blackfeet warriors suddenly crested a hill. They spied him about the same time he caught sight of them. For a moment neither trapper nor Indian moved; then with a sudden rush the war party charged down the hill. Kit yanked his horse around and buried his heels in her sides. The weary animal gave a good start, leaping instantly into a full gallop. There was no place to run to, so Kit just pointed the animal's nose in the direction of the wagon tracks and, whipping the long ends of his reins, urged her onto greater speed.

He had only one chance, and that was to shake these murderers off his trail. But how? Kit glanced over his shoulder again. The Blackfeet were closer. His horse was flagging. He lashed the horse with the ends of his reins relentlessly, demanding of the mare everything she had to give. She stumbled, then recovered. There was nothing ahead but wide-open ground, while behind him certain death was slowly closing in on him.

KIT CARSON

OREGON TRAVAIL

DOUG HAWKINS

LEISURE BOOKS   🄻   NEW YORK CITY

For James Doyle
with whom I have shared many a cold tent
and warm camaraderie.

A LEISURE BOOK®

June 1999

Published by

Dorchester Publishing Co., Inc.
276 Fifth Avenue
New York, NY 10001

ISBN 0-8439-4548-6

ACKNOWLEDGMENTS

My sincerest thanks to the late Dr. Thomas Edward, who so graciously allowed me to roam freely through his rare and valuable collection of monographs by that nineteenth-century Native American scholar, Professor W. G. F. Smith.

OREGON TRAVAIL

Chapter One

Strange.

Kit Carson drew rein and sat there for a long, thoughtful moment upon his coyote dun mare in the dappled light beneath the grove of quaking aspen. His wide, beaver felt hat with an eagle's feather in its silk band was pulled down low to keep the sun's broken light from his pale blue eyes as they narrowed searchingly toward the bright valley before him. Overhead, a pair of hawks made lazy circles in the warm updrafts. At the valley's far end, four deer cropped the tawny grass. A fly buzzed annoyingly near his left ear.

Mighty strange.

The leather straps of a hunting bag and powder horn slanted across his new calico shirt. A brace of Hawken pistols and a tomahawk were thrust under a wide belt, while a butcher knife in a fringed sheath hung at his right side. Many trappers of Kit's ac-

9

quaintance had adapted the Indian style of breech-clout and leggings, but this mountaineer still favored full buckskin britches that fell over the tops of moccasins of smoked buckskin.

He carried a long J.J. Henry rifle, presently resting across his legs. It was stocked to the muzzle in straight walnut, trimmed in iron, and had but a single trigger. There was nothing fancy about the Henry. Its wood was scuffed and nicked and patched about the wrist with rawhide; a workingman's rifle carrying thirty-two balls to the pound; solid, dependable, and in Kit's hands deadly accurate out beyond two hundred yards.

Tied to the back of his saddle, among his bedroll and saddlebags, were a woolen poncho and a new buffalo-skin coat. He had purchased the coat at the rendezvous to replace the one he had lost that spring. Inside the saddlebags was a small pouch of gold coins, what was left from the sale of the beaver he and his brigade had trapped that previous winter. Kit had made a valiant effort to save some of the money this year. He had forsaken drinking and gambling, and buying too many gewgaws for his new bride, Waa-nibe, an Arapaho maiden he had taken to be his wife. It was the first money he had ever saved.

Marriage does that to a man, Kit mused. He grinned just then, sitting there, studying the open land before him. He had seen it happen to others—to Joe Meek when he wed Umentucken, to Jim Bridger on taking a Nez Percé wife.

Gray Feather had been proud of him too. Gray Feather, half Ute, half English, and all Harvard College-educated, was always carrying on about putting a little money away for a rainy day. Well, Kit had managed to put almost sixty dollars away. Apparently some of Gray Feather's frugality had finally rubbed off.

Ahead of Kit lay a long valley, circled about with the forest like the fringe of hair on a bald man's scalp, but down through the middle of it there was only low mountain grass, stiff and brown this late in the summer. Open country made Kit nervous when he was traveling alone—well, almost alone.

"Why are we stopping, Mr. Carson? You suspect there might be some danger ahead? Indians maybe? Sioux?"

Kit glanced over his shoulder. Reverend William Pritchard was watching him with worried eyes. Pritchard wore dark woolen trousers and a white cotton shirt, open at the throat and sweat-stained. His black frock coat was tied behind his saddle along with his saddlebags. A pair of mules carried all of the preacher's earthly possessions, diamond-hitched to *aparejo* packsaddles. Kit knew little of the man except that he was a widower, with a son living in Santa Fe. He had come to preaching late in his life, having spent the better part of twenty years a physician and surgeon back East.

"Sioux? Not likely, not here. Bannock maybe, Snake too. Some Nez Percé and Blackfoot. But no Sioux."

"When I came north with Mr. Cassin, he was always on the lookout for Comanches, or Arapaho, or Sioux."

"Plenty of them Injuns all up and down the eastern side of these here Shining Mountains, and Mr. Cassin knows his business. But now we're too far north for the Comanch, too far west for Sioux and Arapaho, Reverend." Kit returned his view to the tracks in the ground next to his horse's hooves. The wheel ruts from Eliza and Henry Spalding's and Narcissa and Marcus Whitman's wagons were plain enough. He had had no trouble following them since leaving the campgrounds of the yearly rendezvous earlier that week. Now there was a new set of tracks, and these were what had caught his eye and brought a sudden, wary tingle to his spine. Pony tracks. Unshod. And the riders of those unshod ponies had by chance happened upon the Oregon-bound missionaries, and were now trailing them.

The missionaries were being guided to Oregon under the seasoned hand of Thomas McKay. He was the son of Alexander McKay, one of the Astorian partners, and son-in-law of John McLoughlin, the Hudson's Bay Company factor at Fort Vancouver. McKay had established Fort Boise a few years before, and Kit had had a few business dealings with the man and trusted him. McKay was quick as a mountain lion and smart as an old hoot owl. When it came to the ways of the Indians, Thomas McKay knew which way the stick floated, and there was not a higher regard a man of the mountain could earn than that. The immigrants were in good hands, but just the same, there was no way McKay could know that a band of Indians had picked up his trail.

"Your friend, Reverend Spalding, and the others are being followed."

Pritchard's eyes rounded. "So it is Indians, isn't it?"

"The signs say maybe, and maybe not. Plenty of white men ride unshod ponies this far from any blacksmiths. But my gut tells me these riders are redskin."

"What tribe?"

"Can't say yet."

"Could they be friendly?"

Kit looked back. Concern was deepening upon the preacher's sunburned face. "They could be, but I wouldn't count on that being so," he said soberly.

"Then we must hurry on and warn them," Pritchard declared.

Kit studied the long valley again. The tracks of the wagons and their followers headed straight across it. Kit pondered the matter. The trace was at least two days old and he judged that if there was any danger, it would be ahead of them, not lying in wait among the trees that fringed this pleasant valley. . . . At least he hoped so.

"What's that saying about fools rushing in?"

Pritchard frowned. "They have to be warned."

"McKay has more mountain savvy than most men I know, especially when crossing Injun country." Kit kept his own deeper concerns private. "Just the same, we'll pick up our pace some, Reverend." Checking the caps on the nipples of his rifle and pistols, he softly clucked his horse ahead, following the tracks down through the middle of the valley.

They stayed on the tracks all that day. At one point the riders had dismounted to water their animals in a small stream. From the moccasin imprints left on the muddy bank, Kit learned it was a band of Black-foot warriors dogging McKay and company. He judged their number to be fifteen to eighteen.

Late in the day the tracks suddenly veered off the

13

immigrants' trail. Kit and Pritchard stopped and hunkered down over the signs, scratching their heads at the Indians' unexpected change of direction.

"This is good news," Pritchard said, delighted. Then he screwed up his lips and peered intently at Kit. "But you don't look too happy about it, Mr. Carson."

The sun was lowering toward the west, the heat of the day giving way to the coming evening. Mountain nights were almost always cool, even in late July. Pritchard had already shrugged back into his black coat, and it would not be long before Kit would untie the wool poncho from his saddle.

"The Blackfeet love to fight, Reverend. They'll commence to scrapping with any stranger just for the sport of it. It ain't like them to break off like this. Not without a good reason. Something must've pulled them away."

"Well, perhaps that is so, Mr. Carson. But does that matter to us?"

"It might. Depends on what it was that caught their attention." Kit frowned. He didn't like loose ends, especially when there were Indians dangling from them. He stood and peered to the north. The land here was mostly open, stretching away for miles, with small islands of pine and aspen scattered about it. Far away a herd of buffalo dotted a hillside just below a line of trees. The Indians' tracks headed off in that direction. Maybe they had seen the buffalo too and figured hunting food was more profitable than trailing a bunch of Oregon-bound immigrants.

Or maybe it was something else. . . .

For the moment, at least, it appeared that

McKay and his company of travelers were out of danger. Kit was anxious to catch up with the caravan and place Pritchard in their care. Pritchard had traveled up from Santa Fe intending to join the missionaries at the Ham's Fork Rendezvous, but he had arrived three days late. The immigrants had already left. Kit had been preparing to leave with Lucien Fontenelle and a hundred other men, bound back to the Yellow Stone country and another season of trapping. But at the last moment he had agreed to help Pritchard catch up with the party he had missed.

"I say good riddance and let's push on, Mr. Carson."

As eager as Kit was to be done with this job and on his way back to the other trappers, he was just as curious to learn what the Blackfeet were up to. "I'll get you to your friends soon enough, Reverend Pritchard." Kit took up his reins and swung back up into the saddle. "But first I'm gonna take a gander at what these Injuns are up to."

"Is this really necessary?" Pritchard asked impatiently.

"You coming or not? We're gonna lose daylight in another hour."

Pritchard frowned, then gathering up the lead ropes of his two mules, climbed back atop his horse, and fell behind Kit. They started across the open country. The tracks Kit followed went past three or four stands of aspen and pine trees. As they drew near to one of the scattered islands of trees, the tracks suddenly stopped, as if the Blackfeet had chosen this place to wait. But wait for what?

Kit circled the trees. On the other side he drew rein all at once and sat there staring into the dark-

15

ening sky at the wheeling flock of ravens. Some of the birds were settling into the branches of another distant grove of trees, while others were fluttering to the ground a little beyond it.

Pritchard sat there a moment, his head tilted back, his mouth suddenly open. "What does it mean, Mr. Carson?"

"It means we found what it was that pulled them Indians from off the trail of your friends," Kit replied.

Coming around the second island of trees, Kit stopped and stared at the sight before him. He had judged it right. This was what had drawn the Blackfeet off Spalding and Whitman's trace.

"My God," Pritchard breathed behind him, and his hand dove into the pocket of his jacket for the little black book that he kept there.

Before them lay eight bodies, horribly contorted upon the brown grass in their mutilated death. Kit's keen eyes instantly scanned the darkening landscape for any signs of danger, but other than the flocks of black cawing birds, winging overhead and scolding the two travelers from nearby branches, nothing else moved. He stepped down to the ground, holding his rifle ready as he advanced toward the bodies. There were two women, a young boy, two little girls, and three men, one particularly old. They had only been dead a couple of hours, which meant the Blackfeet were still in the neighborhood.

Pritchard was shocked into silence by the scene. Finally, he gulped down a knot in his throat and said softly, "Such violent, vicious deaths, Mr. Carson. Such a horrible way to die."

Kit frowned. "Don't rightly know of too many

16

good ways to meet your Maker, Reverend, except maybe passing on while warm and asleep on your bed."

"The Blackfeet did this?"

Kit nodded, then stalked around the killing grounds, studying each of the victims.

"Why would they do this . . . to their own?"

"Own? They're not thar own, Reverend," he said, pausing to look at the old man. Three arrows had pierced the man's chest. His throat had been slit and his belly opened up and intestines cut out. "These here are Snake Injuns—Shoshoni they're called. Them and the Blackfoot are mortal enemies." He moved on to peer down at one of the women. The men and women had been scalped. The Blackfeet had cut away the women's breasts and the men's private parts. Even the boy had been mutilated. Only the two little girls seemed to have been put to death quickly and then left alone.

Kit glanced up at the darkening sky. He did not want to remain here after dark. The scent of death would soon be attracting other animals, ones that were more dangerous than a flock of ravens. Wolves and coyotes would soon find them, and maybe even a grizzly bear or two. It would be smart to be long gone from this place when that happened.

Pritchard seemed to be struggling inside as he stared at the brutal deaths before him. Kit said, "If you get to feeling woozy in the stomach, it's no shame, Reverend."

Pritchard remained quiet, his ruddy face paling. He was a big man, fully six feet tall, and broad across the shoulders. But the sight of such gruesome death could bring even the brawniest to their knees. Even Kit, seasoned as he was to the ways of the mountains and the Indians that lived in them, was not unaffected by the cruel and violent death here.

"We best get moving. Nothing more we can do for them, unless you want to say a prayer or something, Reverend."

Pritchard shook his head and managed to say, "Too late for prayer here, Mr. Carson, except for the comfort of their families."

"Looks to me they *were* family. Two families, I'd make it, traveling together. That old one thar must have been a grandfather. Maybe to those two women. The men likely were husbands, and between them they had three children."

"Why? Why would those Blackfeet do this? Certainly these people did not provoke it. Not traveling with children as they were."

"Blackfeet don't need a reason, Reverend. It's just thar way."

Stunned, Pritchard stood there a moment longer; then his hand flew to his mouth. He wheeled around and rushed toward the nearby stand of trees.

Kit listened to the violent heaving coming from the darkening trees as he gathered up the reins to their horses and mules and led them away from the bodies. In a few minutes Pritchard's retching ceased. Kit waited patiently in the growing gloom, anxious to be away from there. They would have to make camp once he put these killing grounds far enough behind them. He wondered where the Blackfeet were now. If he didn't miss his guess, he'd say they had gone back to following the missionaries. He was certain he'd pick up their trail again in the morning, just about where the Blackfeet had veered off the immigrants' trace. More than ever now, Kit knew that McKay and the travelers in his care had to be warned.

The deaths of these two families had brought thoughts of his new wife sharply into focus. His heart was at once pricked with a pang of loneliness and at the same time put at ease knowing that Waanibe was at that moment safely with her own people, the Arapaho. Loneliness was not a stranger to Kit, but this time it was of a different sort than any he had experienced in the past, in his bachelor days. Back then it was a hankering for the camaraderie of men cut from his own cloth, or the pretty señoritas in Taòs who always flocked to the fandangos. But this was a deeper sort of longing, and very private—not something he cared to speak about casually to just anyone. But it was a feeling he could share with the other married mountaineers who had left wives behind for a season of trapping.

The line of trees far to the west was now completely black. It suddenly occurred to Kit that he had not heard a peep from Pritchard since the last of his heaving had ceased. Caught up in his own thoughts as he had been, he realized now that he did not know how much time had passed.

"Pritchard? Reverend Pritchard?" he called, not too loudly.

Only silence.

Kit came instantly alert. Maybe the Blackfeet hadn't moved on as he had first thought. What if they had spied him and Pritchard from a distance and had crept back for more sport? Kit swung his rifle toward the stand of trees, his eyes trying to penetrate their thickening blackness.

Nothing moved in there. Pritchard should have been out by now. He should have at least answered his hail.

"William!" he called, louder this time, only to be answered by the whisper of the wind and flutter of black wings settling among the branches for the night.

Chapter Two

Fearing the worst, Kit crouched low and rushed toward the grove of aspen trees, rifle ready, senses suddenly alert, and every nerve tingling as they went to a hair-trigger set. He imagined a swarm of Blackfeet bursting from the dark cover, with poor Reverend Pritchard even now dead. That Kit had not heard anything meant nothing. Blackfeet could move as quietly as a summer breeze, and strike as violently and suddenly as a Rocky Mountain thunderstorm.

He slipped into the trees, relying now more on feel than sight as he moved forward. He resisted the urge to call again, knowing that to do so would instantly pinpoint him for the Blackfeet—if indeed they had returned. From long years of practice, his moccasined feet settled noiselessly upon the leaf-littered floor as if possessing the night-seeing eyes of a cat. His ears caught every sound—which at the moment came only from the birds settling in for the night.

Then there was something else.

Kit froze and listened.

From deeper in the trees came a muffled sound that he could not identify. It was something like the low whine of an animal . . . but what sort of animal? Suddenly footsteps came crashing through the darkness toward him.

Kit swung his rifle around.

The dark form came to a sudden halt, a startled cry leaping from his throat.

"Pritchard!"

"Mr. Carson!"

In the deep gloom of the trees the two men stared at each other. Pritchard lowered his view to the rifle nearly prodding him in the belly.

Kit lifted the muzzle. "I got to worrying about you, Reverend. I had a notion that the Blackfeet might have come back and lifted your scalp. . . ." Then Kit made out the shape of a dark bundle that Pritchard was carrying in his arms. He could not identify it at once, but something in its silhouette was familiar. "What have you got thar?"

"Let's get out of these trees," Pritchard said excitedly, "and I'll show you."

Back out on the plains the night sky was only marginally brighter than the gloom inside the trees, but it was enough difference for Kit to see what it was that Pritchard had found.

"That's a cradleboard!"

"It's a baby!" Pritchard declared.

"Well, so it is," Kit said, lifting away a corner of a

rabbit-fur blanket. The little face stared back at him, dark eyes wide and wondering, a small whimper from drooling lips. Indian children were taught from birth not to cry, and this little one was trying desperately to hold back one powerful wail. "He . . . or she . . . must belong to one of those two women."

"She must have hid him from the Blackfeet," Pritchard surmised.

"Reckon she did."

Pritchard shook his head, and there was a deep sadness in his voice when he spoke. "Oh, the desperate lengths a mother will go to to protect her children. She must have known they were going to die. Oh, the senseless killing. The inhumanity of it all!"

"How old you reckon he is?" Kit asked.

Pritchard studied the tiny face buried deep within the dark folds of deerskin and rabbit fur, then shrugged his shoulders. "It's been a long time for me, Mr. Carson. My children are all grown and on their own. But if memory serves me, I'd hazard a guess that this one is maybe six or seven months old."

"Not even a yearling yet."

Pritchard nodded.

"Cute little fellow, ain't he?"

"All babies are cute, Mr. Carson," he replied, grinning and making unintelligible baby babble for the infant's benefit.

Kit frowned. "This little fellow has been in that stand of trees a long time. Reckon he must be a hungry little crittur by now."

"He'll need milk."

"I haven't got any milk. Got some jerked venison and some peaches."

"No, no, no. That will never do, Mr. Carson."

"Whal, then, what will a tiny little guy like him eat, Reverend?"

"Milk is all I know."

"But we ain't got none," Kit protested again.

The baby whimpered, trying to hold back, but on the verge of wailing and tears.

"He's gonna start crying any second now."

"Injun babies don't generally cry."

"That's silly, Mr. Carson. All babies cry." Pritchard began humming and swaying the cradleboard in his arms. "We are going to have to find something for him to eat."

Kit glanced around at the bodies lying there. "We'll work this problem out later. First thing we gotta do is find us someplace to bed down for the night, before the wolves show up." It was likely that many other scavengers would show up too, and Kit did not want to be anywhere near these dead bodies when they did. The sight of the butchered bodies was unpleasant enough. He did not want to think about what these dead Indians would look like come morning after a night of feasting by the local wolf, coyote, and badger population, not to mention the ravens again. They mounted their horses. Pritchard held onto the baby as they started back the way they had come.

Backtracking, Kit rounded a distant island of aspen trees and made camp on its far side. He built a small fire against some rocks so that the light of it did not show across the open country beyond. He put on a pot of water for coffee, and sliced into the lump of jerky that he had brought along.

Finally, the baby could bear his hunger pangs no

longer and began to cry. Kit was almost relieved when the squalling began—not that he cared to listen to it, but the way Indian mothers trained their infants to remain silent under all but the most trying times seemed downright unnatural to Kit's way of thinking.

"The little fellow is famished," Pritchard said, coo-cooing near the wailing baby's face. Then he turned away and in the flickering light of the fire the preacher's mouth screwed up and he pinched shut his nose. "And I think he filled his diaper too!"

"I don't think they wear diapers," Kit said.

"How do they . . . I mean, what do they use for . . . ?"

Kit scratched his head. He was well versed in Indian ways. He could trade with them as shrewdly as he could make war with them. He could speak a half-dozen dialects, and use sign language as well as any native. But babies? This was something he had little experience with.

"Whal, I think they just sort of pack them all about with shredded bark, or leaves, or maybe grass."

"You think?"

"Pull him out of thar and take a look."

Pritchard frowned, clearly displeased with the task before him.

"We got water for washing, and I can find us some leaves to wash him with." Kit hurried into the stand of trees, looking for something to scrub the baby's bottom with. He was anxious to be away from there before the job somehow found its way into his hands. When he returned, carrying a hatful of leaves stripped from the lower branches of an aspen tree,

25

Pritchard had the baby out of the cradleboard and lying upon the grass.

He looked up at the sound of Kit's footsteps, and although Kit could not see the preacher's face well since it was turned from the firelight, he heard the frown in the man's words of greeting.

"He had filled his 'diaper,' all right, only you were correct, Mr. Carson, he wasn't wearing a diaper. Just a bunch of what appears to be fine, soft bark . . . among other things." He waved an arm and continued, "It's all over there for your examination, if you so desire."

Kit grinned. "I'll take your word for it, Reverend."

"By the way, he is definitely a *he*. I can use some of that water and those leaves for my own cleaning, sir."

"Got you, did he?"

"Just waiting in ambush."

"That's just like them Injuns," Kit quipped.

The infant was thrashing his arms and legs, crying.

"Poor little tyke." Kit gave the baby his finger, which was instantly grasped in a tiny hand. "He's wondering where his mama is, and why his stomach is aching so."

Pritchard washed his hands and scrubbed at his jacket with a handful of leaves and some water from his canteen. "I don't know what we will do with him, Mr. Carson. He needs to eat, but nothing we have with us is fit for a child this young."

"What if I boiled some jerky in water?"

"You can try it, but I don't think he will accept it. What he wants most is mother's milk, and that is something we are in short supply of."

Kit tried to give him water from his tin cup, but

the baby turned his head away from it and cried harder. Kit tried swinging him in his arms and singing a ditty . . . all to no avail. "What am I gonna call you, little one?" Kit said, trying his best to comfort the child. "How about Little Chief? You like that?"

Pritchard cleaned the cradleboard, and they swaddled the baby once again in his rabbit-skin blanket, slipped him back inside the leather pouch, and lashed it up tight again. Then, in a familiar place that offered a bit of security, the baby finally cried himself to sleep while the two men looked on helplessly.

Afterward, they spoke in hushed voices, neither one wanting to wake the infant, for the child had nothing to look forward to but more hunger pangs. Asleep, at least, he was blissfully unaware of his predicament.

Kit put a burning twig to the bowl of his clay pipe and puffed out a cloud of smoke. "We got to decide what to do with Little Chief. It's plain he won't last long without milk, and milk is something we're mighty short of."

"The poor tyke," Pritchard said, shaking his head. He thought a moment, then added, "Mrs. Spalding will know what to do with the infant."

"The immigrants are still days ahead of us. Little Chief needs to eat something now." Kit's eyes went to the sleeping baby, snuggled down deep into the cradleboard leaning against the trunk of a tree.

The board itself was of typical Snake Indian design; broadly rounded at the top, tapering toward the baby's feet. Upon it was the soft deerskin pouch that held the baby tightly in place. The contraption was a model of ingenuity. A woman could carry it upon her back or hang it off the side of a horse when traveling, holding the infant safely in place, and in a position where he could watch the world around him. Cradleboards were usually made for the expectant mother by a family member or a close friend, and presented to her at the birth. A baby would usually spend its first year tied inside one, and if the baby was unusually healthy, the mother might use the board again for her next child. But generally, when the child was old enough to toddle on its own, the board was hung high in a tree and left to nature to return it to dust.

In the dark it was hard to be sure, but Kit reckoned that this particular cradleboard was more highly decorated than others he had seen—not that he had ever paid very close attention to such things before.

"Did they have milk cows with them?" Pritchard asked.

"They did, but Mrs. Spalding isn't here, and Little Chief ain't gonna let us forget his tummy is hurting."

"Can appropriate food be had for him out here, in this wilderness?"

"Thar's food everywhar, if a body knows how to go about finding it. For you and me, it would be easy to find. But for a nursing babe?" Kit shrugged. "Tell you the truth, Reverend, I never had to go looking for that sort of victuals before."

Pritchard's eyes lingered long upon the sleeping baby. A smile came to his face, mingling in among all the concern written there.

Kit pondered the problem a moment, then said, "I can always bleed the mules—"

"Bleed the mules? Absolutely not!" Pritchard retorted, displaying a look of disgust. "We will not feed the child blood, for heaven's sake!"

"Cooked blood ain't so bad, not when starvation is staring you square in the eyes."

"That is out of the question. 'I will set my face against the man who eats blood, saith the Lord.' Leviticus seventeen, verse nine—or is it ten? No matter. No, no, no, blood is out of the question, Mr. Carson. We will just have to push on doubly hard in the morning and pray we reach the caravan quickly."

"I don't mean to be disrespectful, Parson, but I reckon when the Good Lord said those words, he wasn't starving or dying of thirst."

The men fell silent, considering the problem.

And as far as turning the baby over to the missionary women, Kit wasn't sure he agreed with the preacher on that either. Sure, the missionaries were traveling with milk cows, and certainly Mrs. Spalding and Mrs. Whitman would know exactly what to do to care for the infant. But was that the best path to follow?

After a while the older man looked over and asked, "Is something the matter, Mr. Carson?"

Pritchard was a perceptive fellow, and Kit had to grin. "Is it that plain?"

"I can see you are an honest man, Mr. Carson. You don't hide your feelings behind a false face like others of lesser character might."

"I don't think taking Little Chief to your friends is the thing to do."

"What do you mean?"

"Whal, he is Injun, not white. He ought to be taken back to his own people, not handed over to white women."

"You'd return him into the hands of the heathens?" Pritchard asked.

"The way I see it, heathen or not, it's whar he belongs, Reverend. Now, I know that you and the others have come clear across the country and out here to bring the Gospel to these Injuns, and I'm not saying that ain't a good thing, but Little Chief thar, he's a full-blooded Snake. He belongs with his own kind, to be raised in thar ways." Kit was thinking of his friend, Waldo Gray Feather Smith, born to a Ute woman and a white father. Although Gray Feather managed to get along passably well in both worlds, he was never completely accepted in either.

Kit saw that Pritchard did not completely agree, but for the moment he raised no objections. Instead, the preacher said, "Tell me, how do you propose to find his people?"

That was a good question, and one Kit did not have an answer to. The tribe this baby came from could be anywhere! They had less chance of finding them than they did of making it to the missionaries. At least he knew how to find *them*. Kit shook his head.

"I didn't think you knew," said Pritchard. "So that really leaves us with only a couple of alternatives. Either we explore every mountain valley and high trail in these parts looking for his tribe, or we make straight for my friends, where we know we can find help and sustenance for the child."

"Much as I hate to admit it, Reverend, those look to be our only choices. I reckon making straight for your friends is what we ought to do, but that still leaves us with two big problems."

Pritchard lifted a questioning eyebrow and waited.

"Your friends are up ahead two, three days march, but Little Chief has got to be fed something soon, and it's a sure bet he ain't gonna take to coffee, or any of that whiskey I brought along. We can probably get the babe to take some water, maybe a bit of broth made of boiled venison, but he ain't gonna like it."

"And the second dilemma, Mr. Carson?"

Kit grimaced. "Thar's still all those Blackfeet who made Little Chief an orphan in the first place. And the way I reckon it, by now they're again on the trail of your friends. We'd be taking that child right back into thar arrows."

Pritchard looked grim. "It appears there is no good solution to our dilemma."

"It appears not. Dilemmas are most often like that, Reverend Pritchard."

Pritchard's hand dipped into his coat pocket and came out with the tattered bible he kept there. "Then perhaps it is time to take the problem to a higher authority."

Kit nodded. "It's safe to say we can use some extra help right now."

Pritchard opened the book, turned it toward the flickering firelight, and silently began to read.

Kit took up his rifle and strolled out to check on their hobbled animals. The night was quiet and cool. Overhead, bats dove and banked and flitted after insects. It was so quiet and peaceful, it was hard to believe that just a half a mile away lay eight mutilated bodies.

Kit frowned as he ran his fingers through his horse's thick mane. What had begun as a simple job of guiding Reverend William Pritchard to his friends had now turned into something else. Blackfeet were in the neighborhood. They had murdered once and were intent on murdering again. If Kit failed to warn McKay about the danger he and his party of missionaries were in, they would be as good as dead. . . .

And if he failed to find some kind of suitable nourishment for Little Chief soon, the natural course of things would surely finish what the Blackfeet had started.

"Mr. Carson!" Pritchard suddenly shouted. There was alarm in his shrill voice.

Kit wheeled back toward the black stand of trees. Little Chief had been startled awake and was crying.

Then Kit heard something else.

A deep bellowing roar rolled heavily from the trees. It was a sound that Kit knew only all too well, and instantly his blood turned to ice.

Chapter Three

Grizzly bear!

The horses knew the fearful sound too! They whinnied and danced nervously in their hobbles as Kit raced back to where he had left Pritchard and Little Chief. As the black wall of trees ahead of him drew nearer, he caught a glimpse of something moving through the darkness to his right. Too small to be a bear, it must have been Pritchard, sprinting for open country like a man with the devil on his tail— and indeed, Kit reckoned that was just what the preacher had!

Another roar shook the night. Kit dug in his heels and came to a stop, looking everywhere at once. He was breathing heavy, his heart pounding. He gave a quick glance to his right. Pritchard had disappeared. In the blackness of night Kit knew the bear could materialize at any moment and any place. His muscles tensed, fingers tightening upon the rifle in his hands. He looked completely around again and saw nothing.

Cautiously Kit started toward the rock behind which they had built their fire. His view shot toward the nearby tree where Little Chief's cradleboard had been propped. He did not see the board, and was certain Pritchard would have grabbed it up as he had fled . . . but where was Pritchard now . . . and more importantly, where was the bear?

Had the grizzly already caught the preacher? Kit didn't think so. It was just too quiet. . . .

"Reverend?" he called softly.

The night shook. Like an apparition rising out of Hell, nine feet of murderous muscle rose suddenly upon its hind legs from behind the rock that hid their campfire from view. It stood there a moment with the flames of the fire glinting red off the silver-tipped fur. It sniffed the air like a hound dog on the scent of a coon, its keen nose discovering what its poor eyesight could not. All at once, the grizzly's beady eyes locked in on Kit, and again the night shook as it roared out its displeasure at discovering him standing there.

There was no profit in fighting a grizzly bear if you didn't have to. Since Pritchard and Little Chief had already fled the scene, Kit could see no good reason for sticking around. He backed up slowly so as not to alarm the bear. But the bear was already riled, and as Kit took his first step, the huge bear came charging around the rock at him.

Kit shoved the rifle to his shoulder, laid its sights behind the bear's shoulder below the hump, and pulled the trigger. The air resounded with the bark of the Henry as three feet of orange flame stabbed out at the bear. Kit's shot was true. The bear faltered in its headlong rush and seemed to step sideways a pace or two at the impact of Kit's bullet. But the giant bear shook off the shock almost at once.

It was no easy thing to stop a charging griz in its tracks, especially one that weighed nine hundred pounds. A mere half an ounce of lead was hardly going to drop a monster like that! Kit dropped the rifle and lit out of there as fast as his legs could pump.

Another roar ripped open the night. A glance confirmed what Kit had feared. Although wounded, the bear was coming on with a swiftness that belied its huge bulk! Kit put on an extra burst of speed, turning his feet toward the shadowy shape of a distant tree standing all alone in the middle of the open grassy plain.

Not daring to look, he had the feeling nonetheless that he was opening the distance. The rifle bullet had slowed the bear's mad rush, and fear had given wings to Kit's feet. Then, in the darkness, his moccasin snagged something hidden in the grass. He stumbled, scrambled to stab out a foot to catch himself, twisted an ankle, and plowed headfirst into the ground. He took the brunt of the fall on his right shoulder.

A shower of pain cascaded through him, and he lay there momentarily stunned. But the sound of hammering paws, and a vision of the four-inch razor-sharp claws at the tips of those paws overcame his pain, and he rolled to his back and sat up.

The bear was not more than a dozen feet off now. Kit was not aware of the pain in his arm and shoulder as his fist wrapped around one of the Hawkens in his belt. Drawing and cocking the piece in one smooth movement, Kit leveled the pistol and fired.

The bullet slammed into the grizzly's skull, jamming its head back into its spine. But powerful neck muscles absorbed the jolt, and the thick bone of its skull stopped the bullet from crashing all the way into the brain. Yet it was a sledgehammer blow and it stunned the already wounded bear, driving it to the ground, giving Kit an instant to scramble to his feet.

He yanked his butcher knife from its sheath and leaped for the grizzly's back. The monster tried to shake him off, but Kit wrapped his left arm around its neck, grabbing a fistful of fur, and clamped down with his legs, locking himself in place. He plunged the knife deep through hide and muscle, its tip searching for a way through the ribs, seeking the monster's heart and lungs buried deep within that mountain of flesh. The bear stood, and Kit felt himself rising high off the ground. A dozen times his knife drove home. He was running out of time. If the grizzly should shake him free now, or decide to roll over onto him, it would be the end of the fight . . . and the end of Kit!

Then suddenly, the mountain stopped fighting. It stumbled and started to topple. The bullets and knife blows had finally done their work. They had cut the bear's strings, and Kit leaped free as the great beast hit the ground. It lay there a moment, shuddering in the throes of death, then suddenly went still.

Kit picked himself up, shaking from the struggle, slowly becoming aware of his own aches. Although it had readily driven the knife into the beast more than a dozen times, now that the danger had passed, Kit's right arm protested vehemently at being moved. His ankle was sore and sent pain up his leg as he put weight onto it. He rotated his arm, forcing it to move while cautiously circling the dead grizzly.

"Mr. Carson! Mr. Carson! Are you all right?"

Reverend Pritchard was trotting toward him, his arms wrapped tightly around the cradleboard. "I'm not as fit as I was five minutes ago, Parson, but I'll live."

Pritchard stepped around the giant bear, momentarily speechless. The baby was not so inclined to silence, and was loudly informing the world of his unhappy state.

"How is Little Chief?"

Pritchard pulled his round eyes off the dead bear, his shadowy face a mask of shock and surprise. "The child is unharmed, and praise the Lord, so are you . . . you are, aren't you?"

"Hurt my foot, hurt my arm. But I'll heal up." He bent for the knife still lodged deep in the bear's back. Bracing a foot against the mound of lifeless fur, he yanked it out. Looking at the bloody blade, he gave Pritchard a wry smile. "Hope this isn't the way the Lord answers your prayers all the time."

Pritchard gave a short laugh. "No telling, Mr. Carson. The Lord works in mysterious ways."

"Help me pull this crittur over onto its side."

"What do you intend to do with it?"

"This here is one fine b'ar skin. It might fetch two, three dollars."

The two men struggled with the beast until they had its belly exposed, and Kit set about skinning it.

Doug Hawkins

When he finished, he rolled the skin into a bundle and he and Pritchard hauled it back to their camp. Afterward he cut a big roast of rump meat and set it on a spit over their fire to cook slowly throughout the night.

Little Chief bawled for an hour before he finally cried himself to sleep again. Pritchard curled up in his blanket a few minutes later, and was soon snoring peacefully. Kit remained awake, massaging his bruised shoulder and tender ankle, thinking about the baby, the Blackfeet, about McKay and the immigrants, tending the fire, listening to the sounds of the night as the moon arched slowly across the sky. Sometime around three o'clock he dozed, only to be awakened an hour later by the squall of a hungry baby.

A faint pink light had crept into the eastern sky. Kit gathered his blanket around his shoulders and carried Little Chief—cradleboard and all—a little way away from camp so the crying would not wake Pritchard. As he strolled from the trees into the open country, he caught a shadowy glimpse of two small animals slinking away from the carcass of the grizzly. Kit grimaced and walked the other direction. He wanted nothing to do with the bear, even though it was stone dead.

"Belly all afire for wanting something to eat?" Kit asked, a hint of steam on his breath in the chill morning air. Little Chief cried all the louder. Kit tried to make baby talk, but that didn't help. He tried bouncing him in his arms, and made a stab at a song he vaguely recalled from his own mother's knees. At the sound of the melody Little Chief momentarily broke off his agonizing wail and stared at

38

Kit with big brown eyes. Then he commenced hollering all the more.

"Reckon thar's only one thing that's going to make you happy, and frankly, I ain't got a clue where to get it for you." Kit looked out across the land, stymied, and irritated with himself that something as simple as providing victuals for a baby should be such a problem to him.

"What you need is a nursing momma, and nothing else is going to satisfy."

The sound of his voice seemed to help, and Little Chief's wailing diminished to convulsive sobs. In the coming daylight Kit noted that the cradleboard was covered all over in fine beadwork, and there was a curious symbol fashioned out of porcupine quills above Little Chief's head. Someone had put a lot of love and care into making it. Someone of considerable wealth, judging by the quantity of glass trade beads that had gone into its construction.

Kit saw that Pritchard was awake with a blanket over his shoulders, hunkered over the embers of their fire.

"Whal, Little Chief, how about we talk this over with the Reverend. Seems to me that three intelligent men ought to be able to figure a way out of this here beaver trap." He strolled back to their camp.

Pritchard glanced up from the fire he was rekindling with a handful of twigs and sticks. "How is the tyke?"

"Right now his belly thinks his throat has been cut."

"If we push hard, how long do you figure it will take to catch up with the Spaldings?"

"Too long, I fear, at least for this little crittur. He's gonna to need some milk, and soon."

Little Chief commenced to bawling again. Kit tried a little water in his tin cup, but the infant wanted nothing to do with it. In desperation Kit took a little bit of the warm drippings from the bear meat onto his finger and put it to Little Chief's lips. The crying became a whimper as he sucked hard, intrigued by this new taste. But it did little to fill the aching hole in his midsection, and in another moment the crying resumed, huge tears running over his chubby cheeks.

"Surely there is something we can use as a substitute for a couple days."

"Thar probably is, Reverend, and any Injun around here, man or woman, most likely can tell you what it is. But I don't know it. Never had a reason to learn." Kit frowned, wishing that his friend Gray Feather had come along on this errand instead of going north with Fontenelle and the others. Being raised among the Utes until he was twelve or thirteen, Gray Feather would likely know the Indian substitute for mother's milk, if indeed such a thing did exist.

"Then we need to push on quickly," Pritchard declared. "Every minute wasted debating the issue is a minute more it will take us to reach Spalding."

Kit still wasn't convinced that putting the infant into the hands of the missionaries was the best thing, but there seemed no clear alternative. "I'll bring the animals in. You break up camp."

Having been startled by the bear attack, the horses and mules had wandered far in spite of the hobbles, and Kit was a good hour rounding them up. The sun was already in the sky and warming the high mountain valley when the men finally saddled up and left. For a while Pritchard carried Little Chief in his arms, but the infant's crying was getting to him.

"I thought you said Indians taught their babies not to cry," he complained after the first hour.

"They do, and most the time you'll never hear a peep out of one 'em. But then, those babies get fed regularly. Reckon thar is only so much Little Chief can endure, and right now he's hurting. Never before has he been made to go hungry. It's all too new to him."

"He is in no real danger—not for going a few days without food."

"Not so long as we can get him to drink some water." Kit turned in his saddle and looked at Pritchard. "But tell me, Parson, do *you* want to put up with that squalling for two or three days?"

The preacher shook his head.

"Whal, neither do I."

They hung the cradleboard off the back of Pritchard's horse, Indian fashion, thinking that might help. It didn't. Finally Little Chief cried himself to sleep, gnawing at his thumb.

But he awoke an hour later, crying all the harder. Kit had to do something. Even if the baby could survive three days without food, he could not stand hearing the baby suffer so.

Their travel had brought them near a herd of buffalo grazing in a wide valley. Far to the north and west, forest rimmed the place, but it was all grass as far as the eye could see to the south and east. The sun was high and hot and the two men had shed their wraps. Kit reined to a halt to ponder the problem.

Pritchard slung sweat from his brow and settled his hat back upon his balding head. "Why are we stopping, Mr. Carson?"

"That crying is about to drive this coon up a tree."

The preacher looked mildly worried. "What do you intend to do?"

Kit looked back at the grazing herd, a plan taking shape in his imagination. "The way I see it thar's only two ways to shut him up. We either gut him or feed him." He glanced at Pritchard and grinned. "Reckon it's gonna have to be the latter."

Pritchard looked relieved, but he said, "We've been through this already . . . unless you have come up with some new ideas."

"Someone once told me that desperate times demand desperate actions."

"Whatever are you talking about?"

"How much rope you got thar, holding your possibles to those mules?"

"Rope? I don't know. Twenty, thirty feet maybe, if you tie it all together."

"Hmm. Whal, reckon it'll have to do."

"Do? What are you talking about?"

Kit swung out of his saddle and tied his horse to a nearby tree. "I intend to get Little Chief a cup of warm milk." He untied the cradleboard from Pritchard's saddle and hung it in the low branches of the tree. "He should be safe thar until we get back." Kit turned at once to the mules, and began untying the ropes from the packsaddles.

"Back?" Pritchard went around the other side and lent a hand. "Mind telling me what you are thinking, Mr. Carson?"

"Thar's only two places I know of to get milk, Reverend, and that's from a goat or cow."

"That's true. That is why it is so important to reach the Spaldings posthaste."

"Posthaste won't be soon enough. I don't know about you, but hearing that baby suffering so is like a knife turning in my gut. I've known poor bull from fat cow in my life, and I know it ain't easy to take. How much harder when you're only a papoose who's just lost his mother and is knowing the bite of hunger for the first time?"

"I agree, Mr. Carson. But where do you find milk in a wilderness?"

"Same place you find it in civilization, Parson." Kit inclined his head toward the herd of grazing buffalo. "A cow. Now, help me off with these ropes."

Chapter Four

Pritchard finally cranked his mouth shut and stared at Kit as if waiting for the conclusion of a joke. But Kit wasn't smiling as he pulled off the rope and coiled it about his elbow. "You *are* serious!" the preacher finally said.

"In a herd that size, this time of the year, thar are bound to be nursing calves. All I got to do is cut one of the cows out, get a loop of rope over the crittur's head, and tie her off to a tree. I reckon a second loop around her hind legs should hold her in place while I milk her."

"Milk her? Milk her! We are talking about a buffalo, for heaven's sake, Mr. Carson!"

"Got any better ideas? I'll listen to anything you have to offer."

"Yes, I have a better idea. I say we hurry on our

way and catch up with Spalding. Milk a buffalo! Why, I have never heard of such a thing!"

Kit gave him a wry grin. "That makes two of us."

"But you might get yourself killed!"

"And so might you."

"Me?"

"Whal, you don't think I'm gonna do this all by myself, do you?" Kit fashioned two ropes from the pieces.

"I really think you ought to reconsider—"

"Nothing more to think about, Reverend." He fixed a loop in one end of each rope, shook one of them out—the longest one—and whirled it overhead a few minutes to get the feel of it. He'd seen the Spanish *vaqueros* use a rope in just such a fashion while herding and gathering their cattle, but Kit had very little experience throwing a rope. That meant he would have to be close before he made his move. He practiced a few minutes, working the rope into a big loop as he swung it overhead. He let it fly a few dozen times toward a standing rock nearby, and soon got the feel of it. But the rock wasn't moving, and Kit had no delusions about his limited abilities to hit a running buffalo.

"Are you really going to go through with this, Mr. Carson?"

Kit looked at the crying baby, then back at Pritchard, a wry grin upon his face. "Little Chief needs milk and I haven't seen a milkmaid in these parts in a coon's age."

Pritchard frowned heavily, then reluctantly nodded his head. "I see you are a man who knows his own mind, Mr. Carson. All right, since you are bound and determined to go through with this, what is it you want me to do to help?"

Kit was looking around at the scattered bushes growing there. He spied one that looked right, and began chopping the branches from it with his tomahawk. As he worked, he said, "Whal, one thing I know about buffalo is they ain't the smartest critturs that God put on his green earth. No, sir. Why, some days you can sit off a hundred yards with your rifle and commence to shooting them one by one, and the herd will just stand thar watching thar numbers bite the dust, and never figure out what's happening. Then again, five minutes later something as simple as a lightning strike a half a mile off will set them a'-stampeeding. Thar ain't no sense to it, but that's just the way them critturs are."

Kit gathered up the branches and tied them together. "I reckon if I move real slow, I can fool them into thinking I'm just another bush. I will try to get close enough to get a loop over a nursing cow."

"Then what?"

Kit grinned. "Then I hold on for dear life."

"You are not strong enough."

"I know that. Thar are some trees scattered about and if I can manage to get a turn or two around one of them, that should hold her."

"It will be a miracle if you should."

"Whal, you would be the one to know about such things, Reverend."

"So, where do I fit in?"

"You'll help work that miracle."

Pritchard narrowed his eyes suspiciously.

Kit went on. "Once I catch me one of them critturs, the herd will likely spook. They'll light out of thar like someone has kindled a fire under thar tails, and this child will be holding onto the end of a rope attached to one of them. I want you to cut her from the herd and turn her toward the nearest tree so as I can get a turn or two about it before she drags me all the way back to Missouri."

"It's sheer folly!"

Kit gathered up his rope and branches. "Be ready to move once I catch me a cow."

"I will do what I can. But both of us getting ourselves killed will seal Little Chief's fate as well."

"Then we'll just have to make a point of not getting killed, won't we, Reverend?" Kit hunched low behind his camouflage of leaves and started slowly toward the herd, moving a few feet at a time, then pausing for long moments. The technique was laborious and the pace frustratingly slow, but anything more would have startled the grazing animals into a stampede.

It took Kit most of twenty minutes to cross the two hundred yards of open countryside to where he was within spitting distance of the herd. They paid him no attention at all as he crept forward. To them he was just another bush, and there was so little of the odor of man upon the wilderness buckskins he wore, that he made the trek without alerting the beasts in the least.

Kit paused and surveyed the huge, shaggy animals before him. Immediately he spied three cows with nursing calves. One was grazing contentedly at the edge of the herd, and it was toward this one that Kit decided to move. The herd was drifting as it fed. Kit had to move faster than he liked to keep up with it, but the buffalo seemed not to notice. When he got into throwing range of the cow he'd singled out, he very slowly removed one of the two ropes from his shoulder. He worked open the loop. He'd have only one chance at snagging the cow. He couldn't afford to miss.

The herd was easing its way to the west, away from where Pritchard was waiting with his horse. Hurriedly Kit moved to keep up with it, dragging the rope behind him. When they finally stopped, he noticed that they had moved a goodly distance away from any nearby trees. That was not how Kit had wanted it to go, but it could not be helped now. The animals settled down to grazing once more. The nursing calf was standing with its mother as she cropped the stiff brown grass. Kit worked the loop through his finger, grabbing it a foot or so beyond the slipknot. He drew in a couple of deep breaths, rehearsed again in his brain exactly what he intended to do next, readied his muscles, eyed the buffalo, gritted his teeth . . . and made his move.

The loop opened up smoothly above his head at the same instant that he stood up. Startled by the materialization of a man in their midst, the buffaloes momentarily froze, their legs straight as lodge poles, eyes staring from deep within their shaggy faces. Their shock came and went in what might have been three heartbeats before the instinct to bolt registered in their dim brains. By the time it did, the loop was sailing out above the head of the cow. She turned and dug in her hooves at the instant the rope came down over her horns. It did not quite make it around her head, but drew tight around those shiny black horns as she lit out with the other animals.

The rope sizzled through Kit's fists as the great animal began her run. He managed to made a couple turns of it around his arm before it ran completely through his fingers. The jolt nearly pitched him off his feet. His shoulders wrenched in their sockets, and at once he was flying after the cow, legs wheeling faster than a windmill in a gale, toes barely touching the ground, while all around him the thunder of hooves pounded in his ears. As the other buffaloes closed in about him, panic momentarily clouded Kit's thought. He imagined hundreds of hooves pounding the life out of him, and he knew he had to keep moving, had to keep up on his feet in spite of the speed at which the cow was running. He forced himself to think clearly. What crazy notion had prompted him to try such a dangerous thing in the first place? Fortunately, he remained near the edge of the stampede where there were glimpses of prairie beyond the dark brown sea of fleeing animals.

He might release the rope and hope that momentum and chance would carry him through the pounding animals and away from their deadly horns and hooves. That would be the smartest thing—if he could only pull it off. But the rope was taut as a fiddle string about his arm and would not let go of him! Kit's lungs had begun to burn, and his legs ached as if they'd marched a hundred miles. He could not keep this up much longer.

The big shaggy beasts rumbled along near him, some even nudging him. The air filled with dust that clung to his nose and throat, making breathing almost impossible.

Like a flock of birds, the herd turned a little to the east as if under the control of a single mind.

Kit turned with it, hardly able to see for the sweat and dirt billowing into his eyes. Time ceased to exist for him, and he had no notion at all how long he had been pulled headlong across the prairie. All he could think about was not tripping while keeping his legs moving faster than they had ever moved before. He could never have run this fast on his own, but with a ton or more of terrified buffalo pulling him along, his body seemed practically weightless!

Then a sound reached down past his numbed hearing. Somewhere inside his head, his brain registered it as the report of a gun going off nearby, but by this time Kit had lost all sense of direction. He blinked muddy sweat from his eyes and licked it from his lips. He had a vague impression that the herd was breaking apart . . . more spacing between the fleeing animals . . . but he couldn't be certain. Ahead, he caught a fleeting glimpse of a tree, but almost immediately the vision was lost in a cloud of dust.

When the cloud passed, the tree loomed nearer. Then he caught an amazing sight. Moving in among the stampeding animals was a man on horseback twirling a black frock coat over his head. It seemed to Kit so odd an apparition just then, that his thoughts drifted slightly from the task of keeping his feet beneath him. He turned his head for a better look.

It was Pritchard, leaning low in the saddle, swinging his jacket, apparently shouting something. But his words were being swallowed up by the thundering hooves all around him.

The animals broke apart even more. This time Kit was sure of it, and now he clearly saw that Pritchard was doing his level best to turn the cow toward the trees ahead. Pritchard was in as precarious a situation as was Kit, for if his horse went down it would be all over for the man of God, regardless of any good works he was attempting now. In fact, Kit mused, his brain half-numbed already, it could only be by the hand of Providence that he had remained aloft this long.

Then all at once Kit was in the open! Still a helpless fish at the end of the line, he watched the last of the nearby animals thunder past as the herd veered back to the west. Now it was only this cow, and Pritchard upon his horse batting at her with the dark jacket . . . and the fast-approaching tree!

As the cow turned, the rope went momentarily slack. Kit's thoughts came back to the task, razor sharp. He dug in his heels. When the slack played out, the sudden resistance yanked the buffalo's head further toward the tree. Then Kit was flying after her again. Pritchard moved in close and whipped the coat out in front of her, neatly draping it over her eyes and hooking it upon the pointed horns. She was blinded, and her pace faltered. Kit had to force his legs to keep pumping. All he wanted to do was keel over and not move an inch for the rest of the day. But now was not the time. He marshaled what little strength he had left and at the last moment sprang to the right. Then the tree intervened between them. He had only a half second to leap back to the left, hop over the rope, make two turns around the tree trunk, and brace his feet against it.

The tree trembled when the cow reached the end of her rope. Kit held on for dear life as the hemp cord smoked around its trunk, slowly coming to a stop. The jolt of it swung the cow around. Kit thought for sure it would snap Pritchard's line. But the rope was still new, bought in Santa Fe only a month earlier, and it held in spite of all the strain. The buffalo tossed her head, trying to dislodge Pritchard's jacket. Finding herself unable to do so, she just stood there trembling, legs stiff, keeping the line taut enough to launch an arrow.

Pritchard sawed at the reins of his horse, bringing it to a stop. For a man of his age, he leaped from the saddle with an amazing agility, and fell to his knees by Kit's side. He stared at Kit as if searching for some deadly wound.

"You all right?"

Kit could not speak at first. His mouth felt as if it was packed solid with prairie dust. He managed to nod his head.

"That was the most damned-fool thing I ever did see!" Pritchard declared, working at untying the rope still wound tightly around Kit's arm.

Kit was surprised by the expletive. In the four days he had been riding with Pritchard, the reverend had never once used a word stronger than *darn*! Kit worked some moisture into his mouth, spat out a stream of mud blacker than chewing tobacco, and croaked, "Next time this child comes up with a fool-crazy notion like roping a buffalo, you have my say-so to go ahead and shoot me."

"There will be no next time, Mr. Carson, I can assure you of that." Pritchard got the rope off Kit's arm and gave it another turn around the tree trunk, putting a knot in it to keep it there.

Kit back, exhausted, taking an account of every aching muscle, and there was a passel of them. He rubbed his arm, pulled up his sleeve, and frowned at the angry red furrows impressed there upon his skin.

"You are lucky that cow didn't rip your arm clean away," Pritchard scolded, but there was deep concern on his face as he took Kit's arm in his soft hands and examined it with the skillful touch of a physician. "Seems there has been no harm done," he said. "Well, Mr. Carson, now that you have caught your cow, what do you intend to do with her?"

He didn't want to think about that right now, but knew he must. Groaning softly, Kit sat up, then stood. His legs wobbled and he staggered like a shipboard drunk, until he straightened up and felt some strength returning to them.

"Milk her," he said.

Pritchard shook his head in amazement. "Have at it, Mr. Carson."

"I intend to, Reverend," he said, unslinging the second rope from his shoulder. "But I'm gonna need your help again."

"I'm into it this far. Might as well see it all the way through."

Kit staggered his way to the cow, all the while shaking out a loop in the rope. She heard him coming and stepped sideways. Kit threw the loop in her path and when she walked over it he yanked it tight around her hind legs.

She bellowed and kicked and pulled harder at the rope still holding her by the horns. Kit fought the rope all the way over to Pritchard's horse and tied it off on the saddle horn. Then he grabbed the dangling reins and led the horse forward, taking up the slack until he had the buffalo held tight between the two lines.

"Just keep her here," he told Pritchard, putting the horse in his charge. He grabbed off the canteen, and from the saddlebag took the preacher's tin cup. Kit took a long swig of water, worked it around in his mouth, and spat another stream of muddy water at the ground. He swallowed a goodly amount of water, before dumping the rest out.

"Look," Pritchard said, pointing at the calf that stood a few hundred yards off, bleating helplessly. The sound of its plaintive call caused the mother to dance anxiously in the ropes.

"Just keep her tight," Kit said.

Pritchard urged the horse back another step.

"Don't want her to work those hooves loose while my head's under her."

"No, of course not. That would be *udder* disaster," Pritchard replied, straight-faced.

Kit looked over and groaned. Then, squaring his shoulders, he marched toward the buffalo.

Chapter Five

Murmuring soft, soothing sounds, Kit advanced toward the captive monster. His easy words didn't seem to calm the frightened animal one little bit, but they were reassuring to himself, and right now he could use all the reassurance he could get.

"Hope you appreciate all I been through to get some victuals for you," he said aloud, thinking of Little Chief. The infant was quite a ways back considering how far the stampede had carried them. At least he was safely tucked inside his cradleboard and hung up in a tree where he would be safe from the roving dangers of the wilderness.

The buffalo snorted, sensing Kit standing there. Pritchard's coat, draped over her eyes, was working miracles keeping her from trying to bolt.

"You just stay still a little while longer and we can both be out of here and on our way, missy." Kit laid a hand gently upon her heaving flanks, feeling her fright. He didn't know which of the two of them was more scared. "Thar you go. Just settle down and this will be over in two shakes of a lamb's tail—whal, make that a buffalo's tail."

The bleating calf came a few dozen paces closer and just stood there watching helplessly. But its presence did seem to calm the big female just a little.

Kit slowly slid his hand down her side and then, eyeing the front and rear legs warily, he reached for a teat. At his touch she danced a jig as best she could, bound up as she was. Pritchard managed to keep the rear rope taut, and all in all, the buffalo had no choice but to stand there and let Kit fill the tin cup with her milk.

He poured the cup into the canteen and repeated the process. After three more times the canteen was nearly full. The milk would likely sour the canteen for water, but the cause was a good one and canteens were easily enough replaced. When he finished, Kit heaved a huge sigh of relief and scurried away from those legs, which, should she manage to break free, could kick and trample the life out of a man as easily as snapping a toothpick.

"You did it," Pritchard said, amazed.

"It was a fool's mission, Parson, and I'm lucky to still be breathing." He glanced at the preacher, adding, "And so are you. That was some fancy riding you did back thar. Throwing your coat over her head was good thinking. Where did you ever learn to cut a buffalo out of a herd?"

"First off, I do not believe luck had anything to do with our success, Mr. Carson. And second, to answer your question, I wasn't always a Minister of the

Word, or a physician, you know. When I was a much younger man, I worked for one of the biggest horse farms in Virginia. The owner was a gentleman named Roderus, and he made a fat living selling harness trotters to well-heeled gents down in the Carolinas. He was a breeder held in high regard. His farm produced some of the finest racehorses and burliest draft animals any man could want to own. Therefore, when I saw that you had caught yourself a buffalo . . . " He paused and let a small grin lift the corners of his mouth. "Or shall I say, when *she* had caught *you,* I just pretended they were horses, and that I was herding them again, like I used to."

Kit's opinion of the man hitched up a notch or two. It was true that Pritchard was a greenhorn when it came to the ways of the mountains and Western Indians, but he wasn't *green* to life.

Pritchard cleared his throat and said, "Now that we got the milk, how do you propose to release that animal without endangering yourself?"

"That's easy." Kit capped the canteen and set it aside. "Undo the rope from your saddle, and when I give the word let it go."

Kit slipped his butcher knife from its sheath and approached the animal again. He waited until Pritchard was ready, then quickly snatched Pritchard's coat from off her eyes while at the same time slicing the rope around her horns. "Now!" Kit shouted, scrambling back.

Pritchard dropped the rope. Suddenly unfettered on both ends, the buffalo wheeled away from the men, kicking the rope free of her hind legs as she broke into a run. The calf picked up Mama's cue and took off after her. In a couple of minutes they were but two black smudges on the wide prairie, high-tailing it after the herd, which had disappeared far to the east.

After gathering up the canteen, the men walked back to where they had left Little Chief hanging in the tree. They found the baby right where they had left him, sound asleep. Kit almost regretted having to wake him, but Little Chief had to be fed, and they had to be on their way. The more immediate concern of finding nourishment for the baby had forced Kit to put the problem of the Blackfeet to the back of his brain. Now that they had solved the first problem, the urgency to reach McKay and the pilgrims, to warn them of the danger, once again became Kit's main concern.

Pritchard lifted the cradleboard out of the tree, and sat in the shade with it on his lap while Kit poured some of the still-warm milk into the cup.

"He will have difficulty taking it in that manner," Pritchard advised.

"I don't have any other way to give it to him, Reverend. If he's hungry enough, he'll take it this way." Kit softly stroked the infant's cheek. "Wake up, Little Chief. Got something good for your belly here."

Little Chief's dark eyes fluttered open. Immediately his empty stomach ordered a wail to his lips. Kit saw it coming and was faster on the draw, beating the cry with the tin cup. He tilted it just enough for the baby to get a taste of the milk. The cry choked off in his throat as the papoose sampled the fare. Then Little Chief made a face and shook his head. The taste was all wrong. Kit feared he would reject the buffalo milk. Hunger, however, overruled the infant's culinary preferences, and awkwardly he began nursing at the rim of the cup, dribbling about as much of the hard-won liquid down his chin as was getting to his tummy.

Little Chief worked at it with the diligence of a beaver, something to be admired to Kit's way of thinking. In a few minutes the cup was empty and Little Chief puckered up and began to cry again. This time Pritchard knew what was wrong. He put the infant to his shoulder and patted a man-sized belch from the little fellow.

The two men grinned at each other as if it had been they who had burped. Afterward, the baby took a little more of the milk, and then for the first time since they had rescued him, he smiled and cooed.

The sound of that contentment was enough to swell a crusty mountaineer's heart. To hear the little giggle was worth all the trouble Kit had gone through. And from the look on the older man's face, Pritchard was thinking the same thing.

"That satisfied him," Pritchard said, beaming like a proud father as he hugged the cradleboard, slowly rocking it in his arms.

Kit sniffed the air. "Smells like he left something in thar for us to see to."

The men cleaned him and the cradleboard, then put it all back together again. They repacked the mules, reloaded Pritchard's saddle pistol, and were preparing to leave when all at once Kit stopped and stared toward the north, where the forest stood closest.

"What is it?" Pritchard asked, seeing the mountaineer go stiff. His eyes narrowed and swept the rolling land that rose and descended like waves on

59

an ocean, until finally they met the forest not very far off.

"Thought I saw something move among those trees, Reverend."

"What?" Pritchard drew his pistol from the saddle holster as Kit reached for the long rifle leaning against the tree.

"I don't know. I thought I saw movement . . . or maybe nothing at all."

"Animal?"

"Not sure." Kit nodded at their horses, his wary view scouring the land to the west. "Saddle up, Preacher. We've tarried here too long." The hairs at the nape of his neck had begun to stiffen and tingle, and that was never a good sign. Quickly Kit ticked down a roll call of possible dangers. High on that list was Indians, and right at the very top were the Blackfeet who had butchered Little Chief's family.

Pritchard started for his mount, then gave a startled yelp, and his finger shot toward a nearby ridge off in a direction neither he nor Kit had been watching.

Kit cursed to himself at being so easily fooled. He'd figured any attack would be from the trees. But this war party had been smarter than that. They had circled around and followed a fold in the land. When they emerged, they were immediately upon the two men, drawing a semicircle of half-naked riders around them like a noose tightening about a condemned man's neck!

"Blackfeet!" Pritchard declared, raising the horse pistol.

With two dozen arrows nocked in two dozen bows, to fight would be suicide. And Kit saw right off that they weren't Blackfeet, and it wasn't a war party after all. He grabbed Pritchard by the sleeve. "Hold on thar a minute, Reverend. Fire that horse pistol and you're likely to send us both on to the hereafter."

"You saw what they did to those poor Indians!" There was panic in Pritchard's voice.

The noose tightened as sun-darkened riders closed slowly, cautiously, even though they vastly outnumbered the whites.

"These ain't the same ones, Preacher. Thar not Blackfeet. And thar not wearing war paint. This might just be a hunting party."

"If you say so," he said nervously. "You are the expert who is suppose to know about these things." Then he shook his head, and there was remorse in his voice when he next spoke. "Whatever could I have been thinking of anyway? I did not come out here to shoot Indians, but to bring them the Gospel."

"You reacted like most men might, startled and all like we was."

The Indians drew to a halt a dozen yards out, and sat there studying them. Then two riders came forward. One was holding a bow. The second man's bow was slung across his shoulder, and he carried a long lance with an iron point. Bowholder was a short, thickset man. He had not seen starving times in the near past. Lanceholder, on the other hand, was a tall, slender fellow with cords of long muscle stretching down arms and legs, his bronze skin gleaming in the sunlight. He had a long, sharp nose, a tight unsmiling mouth, and wore a single eagle feather in his topknot. Both men wore scarlet breechclouts and buckskin leggings with knives upon leather belts.

Kit wasn't certain at first of the tribe. He knew for certain they were not Blackfeet. They could be Bannock, or even Snake.

Kit shot a glance at the symbol upon the blanket beneath the flimsy rawhide saddle upon which Lanceholder rode. Kit had wondered about the fancy beadwork upon the cradleboard, and the symbol fashioned there of quills and glass beads. Now he understood. The two were the same. It was a clan sign.

When the Indians drew to a halt, Kit glanced at the babe in Pritchard's arms, then at the preacher and said softly, "Thar Snakes, and if I haven't missed my guess, kinfolk to Little Chief."

Pritchard said, "What shall we do?"

Lanceholder's dark gaze lingered upon the mountain man a long moment. Kit grinned affably in return and rested the butt of his rifle upon the ground, holding it by the barrel. Being outnumbered twelve to one, he didn't want to give them any reason to be nervous. He had a fair handle on the Shoshoni tongue since the tribe was generally tolerant toward whites and many Shoshoni were regular visitors to the annual rendezvous, although Kit could not remember ever seeing this fellow, or his more hefty friend, at any of the gatherings.

The warrior's view shifted and briefly touched upon Pritchard. Then it fixed on the cradleboard. Instantly his eyes rounded and the wary, curious look turned murderous.

"Buffalo Pony!" he declared. Thrusting his lance into the air, he gave a cry that instantly summoned the other warriors. Horses pounded and before Kit could blink twice, he was looking into a dozen arrowheads all around them.

Lanceholder leaped from his horse and grabbed the infant from Pritchard's arms. He glared at the man, then at the baby, the murder in his eyes shifting now to deep concern. He spat a question at Pritchard so quickly that Kit couldn't translate it.

Pritchard stood there dumbfounded, riveted by their sudden hostility.

The lance shot forward, touching the preacher's throat. The Indian barked out the question again. This time Kit caught part of it, and it was plain what the Indian was demanding to be told.

"We found the baby," Kit said.

The Indian spun toward the mountain man, fire burning behind his dark eyes. "I don't believe your words, white man. You do not find babies! Where are the others? Buffalo Pony's mother, his aunt?" He clutched Buffalo Pony in one arm and the lance in his other hand, its point hovering near Kit's heart.

"I speak to you true words," Kit said in a broken manner, grasping for the right words, using sign to fill in the gaps. "We found the baby and would have returned him to his people, but we did not know where to find you."

The lean warrior's keen dark eyes narrowed at Kit, attempting to discern truth or lie. Kit went on quickly. "We have done our best to care for the babe, and will be right pleased now if you will take him back to your women. He has not eaten regular in most of two days. We managed to take milk from a buffalo cow, but he needs a woman to nourish him."

"Take milk from buffalo?" The glare turned skeptical before hardening again to flint. "The mother and the aunt . . . my sisters, where are they?"

So that was the deal. Not only was Little Chief—Buffalo Pony—of this tribe, but here was his uncle, and from the looks of it, a man in authority, a chief maybe. Kit frowned, uneasy over the reaction he would get once he told him the truth. But there was no beating around the bush. Drawing out the inevitable could only make matters worse for him and Pritchard. Already the man suspected the women's fate. He was only waiting to hear it from Kit's lips.

"The mother and aunt, and the men traveling with them, are about half a day's ride from here. Thar was an old man and children with them too." Kit grimaced. "Thar dead . . . all of them."

There was a sudden rattle of weapons all about them, but Kit kept his eyes locked upon the Indian who appeared, for the moment, to have ceased breathing. For what seemed an eternity, time stood still. It could have gone either way for Kit and Pritchard just then, and that all depended on what this man did next. Kit read the shock upon the Indian's face, and he sensed the others were reeling from the news too.

"Seize them!"

Warriors leaped from every direction at once. Kit's rifle was snatched away and his arms wrenched behind his back. His pistols, tomahawk, and knife were yanked from his belt. A leather thong bit viciously into his wrist, and the next instant he and Pritchard were shoved back against the tree.

Buffalo Pony had begun to whimper. Lanceholder put the baby in the care of one of the men there, and leveled the lance at Kit.

"I am Hunting Wolf, chief of the Shoshoni. If you do not tell me true words, they will be your last words!"

"I am Kit Carson, and I already have spoken true words to Hunting Wolf. Only the baby lives. All the others are dead."

Rage gripped the chief, but Kit did not flinch from the threat of his imminent demise. To show cowardliness now would surely push the chief over the edge, and death would be only a single spear thrust away.

"We found your people, but were too late to save them. All we could do was save the child."

"I do not believe the words that you say!" Hunting Wolf cocked his arm.

The stout one grabbed the spear's shaft at the last moment. "Wait, brother."

Hunting Wolf shot a look at the shorter man. "He lies, Calling Elk. If they are dead, then it was this white man who killed them."

"Perhaps you are right, but there are ways to be certain. I must ask myself and you this one question. If they did kill Tall Grass Woman and Sleeping Fawn, why have they spared little Buffalo Pony?"

Pritchard had closed his eyes. Now he parted one of them carefully and slanted it at Kit. "What are they saying?"

"The one with the lance thinks we killed Buffalo Pony's ma and pa. The other one, he ain't so sure."

"Buffalo Pony? Is that the child's name?"

"Yes. The tall, skinny one, he's the chief, and the baby's uncle. He's called Hunting Wolf. The heavy one is named Calling Elk."

"He is the baby's uncle? That's just wonderful,"

Pritchard lamented. "You must convince him we did not harm the child's parents!"

"What do you think I'm trying to do?"

Hunting Wolf glared at Kit and Pritchard as Calling Elk continued. "If this is true and they are dead, my sadness is as great as yours, for they are my cousins. Before we kill these two, I want to learn more of what they have to say. Afterward, we can determine the truth in their words."

Slowly the logic of that reached down into Hunting Wolf's distraught brain. His face rigid with restrained rage and dread, he demanded, "Tell me what happened, white man."

"What is he saying?"

"He's giving us a chance to plead our case."

"Make it good, Mr. Carson."

With his hands tied, Kit was hampered, for his grasp of Shoshoni was limited. The finger talk that different tribes used to communicate when language was a barrier was widely understood by most Indians, and a language in itself.

"I will tell you all I know, Hunting Wolf, but you must untie my hands."

The chief understood, and ordered the cords cut.

Kit rubbed his wrists. "We are traveling to meet up with some friends. They are missionaries heading to Oregon. Two, three days' ride ahead. Two days ago I came across the sign of Blackfeet, and saw that they were stalking our friends."

A low murmur worked its way through the listening men. The Blackfeet and Shoshoni were deadly enemies.

"Whal, all of a sudden the devils broke off the trail of our friends, and I figured thar must have been a good reason for them to do that, so we followed them. That's when we come across the women and children, and thar men."

He had their full attention, and that, at least, meant they were weighing his words. "Your family was attacked and murdered by the Blackfeet, Hunting Wolf. But they must have had some warning, for one of the women managed to hide little Buffalo Pony in a stand of trees. Reverend Pritchard, he found the poor fellow."

Kit shifted his view toward the babe in the arms of one of the warriors and grinned. "We named him Little Chief. We wanted to take him to his people, but didn't know where to find you. So, we were taking him to the missionaries where thar are white women who would have cared for a child."

Kit's grin faded. "For the infant's sake, at least, I'm right pleased you and your warriors showed up."

Chapter Six

When Kit finished telling all he knew, the warriors frowned at each other and at him. Some of the men appeared to believe what he had told them. Hunting Wolf was still unsure. Calling Elk finally broke the silence that had settled around them.

"If he speaks true words, my brother, then we must see it with our own eyes."

The chief nodded. "Yes. There is only one way to sift the truth in this. You will take us to them, white man."

Kit had half expected that. At another time the delay would not have mattered much. But there were still the Blackfeet to contend with, and they were closing in on McKay and the Oregon-bound immigrants even now. Kit had to warn them.

"Hunting Wolf. The murderers who killed your family are following my friends. I must warn them. I cannot go with you now."

The lance snapped down again and hovered a moment by Kit's jugular; then it shifted and pressed against Pritchard's shirt. "You will take me to my sisters or he dies now."

"Mr. Carson!"

Hunting Wolf had left him no choice. If he refused, Pritchard would die. If he agreed, McKay and the others might die later. Pritchard's fate was most immediate. "All right. I'll lead you. But we must go swiftly."

Kit reached for the leather thongs binding Pritchard's hands, but Hunting Wolf stopped him.

"He stays. You come only." Turning to his men, Hunting Wolf ordered half to return to their hunting camp with the baby and Pritchard. The rest would accompany Hunting Wolf and Calling Elk.

They hauled Pritchard to his horse and made him mount up. Before they left, Calling Elk went to one of the warriors, a young man with a livid scar down his left cheek, and spoke quietly with him. Then the company of men swung up onto the back of their ponies and started away.

Pritchard craned his neck around and stared over his shoulder at Kit as they led him away. "What are they doing? Where are they taking me, Mr. Carson?"

"They want me to take them to the bodies, Reverend. They're taking you to thar village for safekeeping. You'll be all right until I come back for you," Kit called to him.

Pritchard kept his wide eyes fixed upon Kit as the party of Indians led him away, until finally an intervening fall of land dropped them out of sight.

Kit turned to Hunting Wolf. "I'll take you where you

want to go, Chief, but if your people hurt my friend, it'll be you I'll come looking for. Understand me?"

"He understands you," Calling Elk replied in perfect English.

"So, you speak the white man's tongue."

The thickset man nodded. "Many questions are answered by what men say when they think you do not understand."

"Reckon that's one way to get at the truth." He looked back at Hunting Wolf. "You talk American too?"

"He does not," Calling Elk answered.

"Too bad. Whal, at least you know that I told you the truth."

"We will see," Calling Elk replied flatly.

Hunting Wolf barked an order to his men, and they mounted up.

"My weapons?" Kit asked the chief.

"We will keep your guns," he said, but he returned Kit's knife and tomahawk.

Kit stepped into his stirrup and swung a leg over the coyote dun. "Let's hurry up and get this over with, Hunting Wolf. I've still got to warn McKay about the Blackfeet tailing him." Turning to Calling Elk, he switched to English. "This child's got to tell you, Calling Elk, it ain't going to be a pretty sight."

Calling Elk's face remained a flat, expressionless mask that hid what he was feeling inside. He merely nodded.

Recalling the mutilated bodies, Kit could not be as stone-faced. Grimacing, he turned his animal away from there and started back to the carnage the Blackfeet had left in their murdering wake.

Reverend William Pritchard didn't know if he was to live or die. He rather suspected the latter even as he earnestly prayed for the former. He had left civilization to come to the Far West to minister to the Indians. But he'd never expected to become separated from his white companions, or to find himself alone and a captive of the Shoshonis—the Snake as the men of the mountains called them. Now here he was, hands bound up tight and riding single file in the middle of a line of Indians. His only hope lay in the Shoshonis finally believing Kit's explanation of how they had come to be in possession of the chief's infant nephew.

A warrior who rode behind Pritchard was carrying Buffalo Pony off the side of his horse. The preacher glanced at the infant. The baby was awake and wide-eyed, curiously watching the world roll slowly past him. His was a world of horses and trees and wide vistas as far as the eye could see. A world of crisp mountain air filled with the odors of campfires, pine trees, and last year's aspen leaves decaying upon the moist forest floors. A world whose only clocks were the sun, moon, and seasons; where warm summer days were spent hunting and drying meat; and in the dead of winter only a skin tipi, buffalo robe, and fire kept death's icy grip at bay. Where life was measured by battles between warring tribes or by the long marches between summer and winter camps. Where buffalo hunts and berry-gathering measured its pulse. A life regimented by the passage of seasons and a deep-seated fear of the unknown. Where fables and myths were as real as the cold and heat of the land.

Doug Hawkins

Pritchard frowned. It was just this sort of people he had come west to serve—not the Shoshonis, of course, but the Cayuse farther west. He had corresponded by letter with his good friend Henry Spalding for more than two years concerning the possibilities of going west to work with the Indians. They had planned to meet at the yearly rendezvous. He had joined a wagon train in Missouri bound for the Santa Fe Trail, and spent a pleasant spring and early summer in Santa Fe with his son, Robert, who had recently moved there to open a mercantile business. Afterward, he'd joined up with Harold Cassin, who was organizing an expedition to the mouth of Horse Creek on the Green River.

The weather, however, proved a constant challenge to their travel. It was dreary and rainy most all the way, and the wagons had a hard time of it. Delay after delay slowed them on the muddy trails up the eastern edge of the Rocky Mountains. A wagon broke an axle at the Arkansas River crossing. The travelers had waited nearly a week at the trading post of El Pueblo while a company of men rode sixty miles south to William and Charles Bent's big adobe trading house near the confluence of the Purgatoire and Arkansas Rivers for a replacement part.

As Pritchard recalled that long week of waiting, what had struck him most was the grass and buffalo. Both stretched away to the east as far as the eye could see—clear back to Missouri! The vastness of that ocean of grass was almost beyond comprehension. And the buffalo! Their numbers were endless.

Like the children of Abraham, *as many as the stars of the heaven, and as the sand which is upon the seashore,* he mused, managing a small smile in spite of his predicament.

Once again he began to pray, but a whimper from behind him drew his attention. Buffalo Pony was stirring uneasily, and Pritchard was about to tell them that the child was getting hungry again. But he didn't. They would certainly realize that without him telling them. Besides, he could not speak a word of Shoshoni. That even one of these Indians might understand English was almost beyond hope, but he tagged it onto his list of things to pray for—a list growing longer by the minute!

They rode on with the afternoon shadows lengthening and the sun full in his face. He judged that it had been four, maybe five hours since he had left Kit Carson with the other half of this band of hunters. Reckoning the distance he and Mr. Carson had traveled that morning, Pritchard figured they should be reaching the dead bodies right about now. It would be plain to the Shoshonis then that it had been other Indians and not they who had murdered Buffalo Pony's kinfolk.

At least he hoped it would be plain.

They might kill him anyway for the sport of it, just because he was white. Hundreds of stories of such atrocities had made their way back east. Most everyone had heard at least one or two of them. Some of his acquaintances even knew victims personally. Anything could happen in these wild mountains!

Pritchard gulped down rising fear. This line of thinking was most distressful, and he forced his brain onto other matters. The baby had begun to cry, but suddenly ceased. When Pritchard looked back, he was startled to see that the warrior had pinched the baby's nostrils and was holding a hand over his mouth so that he could not breathe!

Pritchard could hardly believe what he was seeing. The man was trying to suffocate the child! Did no one else notice? The baby was struggling now. Without even considering the consequences of his actions, Pritchard pulled back on his reins and wheeled his horse about.

Instantly he was surrounded. Lances and arrows bristled in his direction. The man suffocating Buffalo Pony had ceased his nefarious deed and had drawn a wicked butcher knife from his belt.

"He was trying to murder the infant!" Pritchard stammered, pointing with bound hands. "I saw him."

The warriors circled about were a heartbeat away from releasing their arrows. Pritchard stiffened, realizing death was as near as the next wrong move on his part. "He . . . he was suffocating the child," he said tightly, fighting down a rising panic, his view leaping from one dark and scowling face to the next.

A young Shoshoni with black hair woven into two long braids down his back, each bound up with a beaded leather band, urged his horse a bit close than the others. He had a short straight nose and a tight unsmiling mouth. He would have been a handsome fellow if it had not been for the puckered scar down the left side of his face. Pritchard's medical training told him that this had been from a wound not properly tended to. Most likely it had been just wrapped in a bandage and left to heal on its own. Too bad, he thought. Properly sutured, the scar would have been hardly noticeable.

He held his bow ready with the wariness of a wild animal upon his swarthy face as he came forward. Pritchard turned to him. He knew this man could not understand his words any more than the others, but he pleaded his case just the same.

"He was trying to suffocate the little one. I saw him."

The young warrior cocked his head, suspicious eyes narrowing and following Pritchard's accusing finger.

"If only I could make you understand," Pritchard lamented. "I was just trying to protect the baby."

Suddenly the warrior's eyes widened, and then he laughed. Pritchard was dumbfounded.

The young man pointed at Buffalo Pony, then at the man tending him, rattled off a quick sentence or two to the others, and the next instant everyone was laughing. In dismay, Pritchard could only stare and shake his head. The weapons lowered and immediately the line re-formed. This time Pritchard was placed several riders forward of the infant, near the head of the column.

As they continued on he tried to fathom what had happened, but drew a blank at every turn. In frustration, he put the matter out of his thoughts. He was alive . . . still . . . and for now that was all that mattered. It wasn't very much later that he became aware of the smell of smoke in the air. From the sudden talk from an otherwise silent crew, Pritchard got the feeling that something was about to happen.

The trail they had been following for more than half an hour had been a tight passage winding steeply through a thickly timbered section of the forest. Now, as they came around a bend in the trail, the trees suddenly parted and before him lay a pretty little valley with a stream gurgling along one side of it, and a village of tipis in its center.

The party drew to a halt and peered out over the tops of the lodges. There must have been forty or fifty skin-covered dwellings, Pritchard reckoned, unable to easily count them all. Some large, some small, some with smoke trailing up out of the open smoke hole, some without. They all seemed to have their door openings facing the same direction. In the open areas among the tipis burned many campfires, and scattered about the village were racks of drying meat.

The village was abuzz with activity. Naked children scampered about playing, while women in long buckskin dresses sat in front of their lodges working. The men he could see were employed in various activities, none that Pritchard could readily identify because they were still too far off. But not so far that he did not hear the sounds of laughing children and barking dogs. Across the valley a small party of men emerged from the forest, leading horses loaded down with deer and elk. Toward the head of the valley was a corral where several dozen horses milled about.

The leader started the party moving again. When they came into the village, all work stopped and every eye fixed upon Reverend William Pritchard. Even the children quit their play to watch this white man being paraded past their tipis, hands bound, wearing a tall, black hat upon his gray head. He tried not to appear frightened, but he had never been very good at hiding his feelings. He managed to grin, but it was a weak attempt at best. They wove their way past the skin lodges, and finally drew to a halt before a large tipi.

The young man with the scar leaped off his pony, stood before the door, and spoke. Announcing their arrival, more than likely, Pritchard surmised.

An older woman appeared from the shadows inside and stood there looking at the men gathered about her front door. Her eyes were glassy and unfocused, and she held her jaw slightly off to one side. Pritchard saw that she was in some sort of torment. Had she broken the jaw? he wondered. Her left palm pressed lightly against her cheek, as if attempting to hold back pain.

The young man spoke quickly, and as he did the woman's eyes sharpened. Her expression went from curiosity to alarm, and then finally to wide-eyed fear.

Then the warrior who had tried to smother the baby unhooked the cradleboard from his saddle and put it into her arms. A tear crawled over her cheek. All at once her dark eyes fixed upon Pritchard. The young man spoke again. She nodded, said something in reply, and quickly ducked back inside with the baby.

The men dismounted and dragged Pritchard from his saddle. They took away his animals, including the two pack mules with all his belongings, and roughly hauled him across the camp, past staring eyes, and through the dark opening into another tipi. Wordlessly, they thrust him down upon a buffalo-skin rug and left him there alone, except for two men who lingered a moment longer glaring at him before turning outside and taking up positions on either side of the door.

Pritchard felt helpless and vulnerable. He knew that these Indians would do with him exactly as they pleased. He could never fight so many, even if he was a fighting man, which he was not. All his life Pritchard preferred the weapon of a quick tongue and sharp wit over the use of knives and fists, and he had become very good at that sort of defense. But what good were words in a place where they could not be understood? No, he was in a hopeless situation. There was little likelihood he could escape undetected, and even if he did, they would just track him down and bring him back.

Now his fate lay in the hands of God, and in Kit Carson convincing these Indians of their innocence.

Chapter Seven

Through the tipi's open door flap, Pritchard watched the village going about its normal life, and except for an occasional glance in his direction, no one seemed to pay very much attention to him. At first the pair of guards remained outside the tipi. They never bothered to look inside and check up on him, and after a while they seemed to become bored with the job and drifted off to chat with friends. Pritchard gave a wry smile in spite of his hopeless predicament. Apparently no one considered him much of a threat, his hands bound as they were. He didn't know if he should be relieved or insulted.

Across the way two men had been talking for quite a while, every now and then casting glances his way and staring. Something in their manner sent a chill up Pritchard's spine. Although communication by words might pose a problem for him, the manner in which a man stood, the way he scowled, and the emphatic gestures of his hands needed no translating.

Pritchard twisted his wrists within the leather thongs that bound them and tried tugging the knot apart with his teeth. In spite of the sheer folly of trying to escape, his thoughts now turned in that direction anyway. Perhaps escape might be possible, but he would attempt it only if he could work his hands free, and to that end he concentrated his energies.

It's at times like these that a man begins to question the roads he has chosen to travel. Pritchard had left behind a good life in the East. He had been—and still was—financially secure. He enjoyed some prestige among his peers in both medicine and preaching. A widower for twelve years, he had left more than one lady teary-eyed at his departure. He looked down at himself. His shirt was stained and threadbare, his trousers likewise, his hands filthy, his shoes scuffed beyond redemption. And beyond these small things, he was being held captive in an Indian village, defenseless, hands bound, with two part-time guards standing nearby.

A wave of despair settled over him. Reverend William Pritchard shrugged it off, recalling why he had left all those things behind. He had sacrificed earthy desires for heavenly ones, the temporal for the eternal. He had come to fulfill the Great Commission; to bring the Good News to these savage people. He was exactly where he had intended to be . . . well, almost.

Then why did he feel so desperate?

Before he could answer that, his attention was

drawn to some movement outside. Across the way a third man had joined the first two. They spoke with much glancing and scowling. Trouble was brewing, he could feel it.

Maybe *that* was why he was desperate!

Pritchard went back to gnawing on his thongs, and he had just begun to work some slack in the leather straps when a shadow darkened the doorway. Startled, he snapped his head up. The late afternoon was turning to dusk with its dusty sunlight slanting sharply across the village. Its warm glow briefly touched the face of an older woman as she stepped inside, accompanied by the young warrior with the scar down his cheek. Pritchard recognized her. It was the same woman who had taken the infant from them earlier. As she stood inside the doorway looking at him, he could see that her eyes were heavy with grief, and beyond that she did not look well. Some ailment was wearing her down.

The woman studied him a long moment before speaking. When she did, the young man at her side translated it into English.

"Grandmother wants to know by what name you are called."

Pritchard was so startled at hearing his own language coming from the young man's mouth that he did not reply at once.

The woman added something and the warrior translated. "It is safe to speak it here. Ninnimbe is not nearby to hear it."

The meaning of that completely escaped him.

The warrior said, "Grandmother is called Laughing Water Woman, in your tongue, and I am Swift Running Antelope."

"You speak English!" Suddenly Pritchard understood why, when he was under their arrows on the trail, this young warrior's words had saved his life. But why had they laughed at him? Did they not believe that the man had been trying to suffocate the infant?

Swift Running Antelope nodded. "I learn the words of the white man from my father, and the white trappers. Trade much beaver and buffalo for cloth, beads, iron knives, and arrow points."

Overwhelmed with relief that at least one person here spoke English, Pritchard mumbled a quick prayer of thanksgiving.

Swift Running Antelope looked at him curiously and said, "You speak to the god of the white man?"

"Yes, yes, I do. I am a minister of the God of the white man. My name is William Pritchard."

He related this to the woman, who showed no reaction to the news. She merely nodded her head and made her reply, wincing at the apparent pain the effort caused her.

"Grandmother wants to know how you find Buffalo Pony. Where is mother and father, brother and sisters?"

The questions opened a floodgate of memories, and the gruesome scene filled his thoughts once again. He grimaced and did not want to speak of it now. "You heard. You were there when Mr. Carson explained it."

"Yes. But she wants your words."

Reluctantly, Pritchard recounted the story, leaving out some of the more vivid details. That they had all died horribly was enough; a litany of the butchery would not be necessary.

Laughing Water Woman listened to Swift Running Antelope's translation, not allowing her emotions to show. But Pritchard saw that the woman was struggling inside to hold them back. He'd heard that stoicism was the Indian's way. Here was stoicism at its zenith, and he couldn't help but wonder if the tables had been turned, if it had been an Indian relating the incident to a white woman, how she would react.

He knew how Edith would have reacted. His own dear wife, God rest her soul, was forever at her emotional wit's end. No doubt it was that point of her character that had led to her early demise. He himself had diagnosed her condition as "nerve weakness." Neurasthenia was the new medical name some were beginning to calling it.

But Laughing Water Woman suffered from no such ailment . . . yet she was suffering, and that was plain to a man of Pritchard's perception.

Finally she spoke, tightly, not moving her jaw any more that was necessary. Swift Running Antelope listened, minutely nodding his head, then turned to Pritchard.

"Grandmother says that if this is true, her daughter's husbands died as warriors should die. Fighting their enemies."

"Maybe. But the women and children, they were not warriors."

"No, they were not. She knows. Your words are a heavy stone. Grandmother carries them inside her now. It will be a burden for a very long time."

"I am sorry, Swift Running Antelope. Truly I am."

Laughing Water Woman spoke briefly to the young man, then turned and went out the door. Swift Running Antelope started to leave too.

Pritchard said, "Does she believe me?"

He turned back. "She not say yet. She waits for the return of Hunting Wolf to hear from his lips what he has learned."

Pritchard's hopes began to dim again. "Could I at least have my hands untied?"

"You will wait for Hunting Wolf. He will decide."

"I see. Tell me of the child. What has happened to him?"

"Grandmother give Buffalo Pony to a mother in the village who will take care of him."

The preacher smiled briefly at the news. "That is good to hear."

The young warrior studied him a moment in the failing daylight, then started out the door again, but Pritchard stopped him one more time.

"Your grandmother. She is not well. What ails her?"

He frowned and turned back. "It is the teeth of an old woman. The yellow poison flows from them."

"Yellow poison? Pus?"

He gave him a blank look.

Pritchard went on. "Have you medicine to relieve the pain?"

"We have the willow bark. And the skunk cabbage poultice, and many others."

"And the results of these remedies are?"

"Sometimes the yellow poison leaves the body. And sometimes it seeps into the spirit and death comes." Swift Running Antelope did not want to pursue the subject further. He wheeled about and ducked out the door flap and disappeared. Pritchard watched after him a long while, his brain shuffling and carefully putting away the memories that had been brought out and dusted off.

As the last of the daylight left the village, replaced by the dancing flames of half-a-dozen scattered campfires, Pritchard saw them again. The three men were squatting on their haunches in front of one of the fires with its light illuminating their faces. More than once they stared at the tipi where he was being held. Something about their manner made his skin crawl.

All at once the men stood and left.

Momentarily Pritchard sat there staring at the place where they had been, wondering what it meant. Then, with renewed drive, Pritchard went back to worrying the leather thongs with his teeth.

Several hours earlier Kit had reined his horse to a stop and squinted hard against the bright landscape to survey the wide plain that stretched away to the east of them. Scattered about it were the islands of pine and aspen, just as he remembered. But he had come upon it first from the east. Arriving from the west as he had now, everything looked different. Kit took a few moments to study the lay of the land and to work out the locations.

"Thar," he said finally, pointing. "Away off in that line of trees. That's where they are, Hunting Wolf."

The company started forward, and as they drew near to the place where the bodies lay, Kit was worried how the warriors would react when they saw them. By this time the bodies must have been heavily scavenged upon. Kit was not looking forward to the sight.

They came around a cluster of trees and reined to a halt. Kit stared a moment, then turned his eyes away. For a long time no one moved, no one spoke. Finally Hunting Wolf dismounted and leaving the horse, walked to the bodies. Two dozen crows scattered to the sky.

Still no one spoke as they all dismounted. Kit accompanied them. Wolves had been by. There was not a lot left that could easily be recognized as human. Except for the scraps of clothing lying around, and the skulls, these could have just as easily been the remains of a butchered herd of deer.

In some ways the sight was easier for Kit to take this time. At least the scavengers had obliterated the mutilations that the Blackfeet had done to the bodies.

Hunting Wolf knelt by one of the twisted forms, touched a long braid of black hair that lay among the torn flesh, then picked up a scrap of beaded buckskin and peered at it.

"Sleeping Fawn," he murmured softly, crushing the material in his fist.

Calling Elk bent and retrieved the broken shaft of an arrow from the grass. "The Blackfeet, my cousin. It is as the white man tells it."

Momentarily at a loss for words, stunned by the tragedy of finding his dead family, Hunting Wolf could only nod his head. The other warriors moved about the grass snatching up more evidence of the perpetrators of this crime. It was quickly clear that Kit had not only spoken true words to Hunting Wolf, but that he and Pritchard had saved the infant as well. But everyone was too grief-stricken to mention it.

Kit walked back to his horse and took it to the trees, where he tied it off and found a place to sit and wait. The Shoshonis were going to have to decide what to do with the bodies. He could have no place in that decision. Afterward, Kit would again make known his desperate need to be away from there so that he might warn his own people of the Blackfeet. But for now the Indians had to be left alone in their grief, and he knew it.

Different tribes took care of their dead in different ways. Some put them up in a burial tree on a special platform. Sometimes, if the dying person requested it, he would be put in a tipi high on a hill. Others took the most expedient course and put their dead in a convenient hole or crevice. Most just buried them, as was the white man's custom. Kit was not sure how the Shoshonis treated the matter, but he was certain that whatever was done here was not going to be the usual way. The corpses were in a terrible state, far beyond what could be conveniently carried back to their village. He suspected that Hunting Wolf would just bury them here.

And that was pretty much what happened. After a small ceremony where the warriors spoke and chanted, Hunting Wolf went about collecting the braids of his family members who had not been scalped. Those braids, together with a scrap of clothing to identify them with, were placed carefully into a parfleche. Then the warriors fanned out into the stand of trees and collected stout sticks. With their knives they flattened the ends into a sort of narrow spade and began digging one big hole. With so many to do the work, the hole grew quickly, and shortly the bodies were laid to rest in earth.

Kit reckoned this would have been a good place for Reverend Pritchard to be, but he did not think these Indians would have appreciated the sort of comfort a man of the cloth brings.

Kit gave them time to bury their dead, and when he figured he had waited long enough, he went to Hunting Wolf.

"I'm right sorry for you and your family. I know this is a time of great sorrow for you and all your people."

He nodded. "There will be much mourning in the village of the Shoshoni."

"Now that you know that I spoke true words, I must go. My own people are in much danger. The murderers who did this to your family are following them now, and I must ride like the wind if I am to warn them in time."

Hunting Wolf nodded again. "I will remember it was you and the white man called Pritchard who saved the life of Buffalo Pony. I will not keep you here any longer. I too must find the Blackfeet, for revenge burns like a coal in my breast, but first we must remain here with our dead."

"I understand. I will return for Pritchard after I have warned the others. Tell him that for me."

"I will speak your words to him. He will not be hurt by my people."

Kit went to his horse, and spied the bearskin tied to the back of his saddle. Not knowing completely why, he untied it and took it to Hunting Wolf. Grizzly-bear hides were of great value to both the Indian and the white man, and Hunting Wolf was surprised when Kit placed it in his arms.

"Little Buffalo Pony is an orphan now, but I know

he will be well cared for by you and the rest of your people. This here gift is small compared to all that he lost here, but I want him to have it."

Hunting Wolf made no reply. None was needed, but Kit felt that right then a bond had been forged between him and the chief, him and this band of Shoshoni Indians. He took his rifle and pistols from one of the warriors, swung a leg over his horse, and dug in his heels.

As if understanding the nature of the emergency, Kit's horse raced on toward the setting sun. Kit ran her hard until the light finally failed. In the darkness he pulled her back to a safe pace and pressed on with only the stars, and a slice of moonlight, to show him the way.

Sometime around midnight Kit made a cold camp. He awoke with the dawn and once again pressed on. There was much lost time to make up, and many miles to cover. He could only hope to reach McKay and the others in time to warn them of the approaching Blackfeet.

Chapter Eight

Calling Elk frowned deeply as Kit Carson rode away from there. In minutes the trapper had shrunk to a mere speck in the distance. When he had finally disappeared beyond a ridge, the stout man shifted his view to the chief.

"Your thoughts are troubling you?" Hunting Wolf asked upon noting the look of concern on Calling Elk's face. He crossed the trampled grass to his cousin's side, still holding the heavy bearskin in his arms. The two men walked together toward the horses. "I know that your heart is heavy, like mine, like all the men here."

"Yes, it holds much sadness," Calling Elk replied. He narrowed his eyes at Hunting Wolf and said, "But I must know. What are your plans now?"

"My plans? What else? We will make war with the people who have done this to us." Anger flared suddenly in his voice. "We will have our revenge for these deeds!"

At the horses, Hunting Wolf tied the gift behind his rawhide saddle.

"When?" Calling Elk asked.

"When we return to the village and gather all the strong men."

"And what of the white men?"

Hunting Wolf considered his cousin a moment.

Calling Elk went on. "It is because of our troubles that Kit Carson was not permitted to ride and warn his people when he still had time. Now he goes alone, to face the murderers of *our* people." Calling Elk paused to let that thought sink in.

"Speak fully on this matter," Hunting Wolf prodded when his cousin fell silent.

"Only this. Kit Carson rides to fight a battle that is rightfully ours. You asked me to speak fully, so I will. Our place is not here with the dead. The dead have gone on. Our place is with Kit Carson, to fight the enemy of our people who have done this. You wish to return to the village for the young men. This is wise but unnecessary. We have strong young men here. Why do we delay? I say we hunt down the enemy now. Not later."

Slowly Hunting Wolf nodded his head. "You have the wisdom of our father, Coyote, my cousin. There is no question that we have chosen our medicine man well." He glanced toward the darkening horizon where Kit had disappeared, then turned and called one of the warriors over.

"Broken Hoof, this you must do. Ride swift, like the eagle flies. Return to our village. Tell what you have seen here. Say to the people that Hunting Wolf says the man called Pritchard is to be released and given honors. Then gather the warriors with all their arrows and lances. We will cross the river at hurling-waters-leaping to fight the Blackfeet. Follow swiftly on our trail and together we will crush our enemy."

Broken Hoof swung up onto his pony and put the animal into a gallop in the direction of the village. Hunting Wolf gathered the remaining warriors around him and announced his intention to make war with the Blackfeet at once. To a man there was agreement on this, and the heavy weight of their grief was instantly put off, replaced with the fire of the coming battle.

As the men gathered their weapons and went to their horses, Hunting Wolf stood over the large grave, peering at the mound of black earth that marked the place where his family lay. Calling Elk came up quietly behind him.

"After many days we will come back to this place, my cousin."

"No. You have already said it. The dead are not here. They have gone on. There is nothing here to come back to. Soon the snows will fly and cover the land, and we will move to our winter camp. Then the grass will grow. After two winters there will be no sign of this place. It is the way of things." Hunting Wolf drew in a deep breath and let it out slowly.

Calling Elk remained at his cousin's side until he was ready to leave. Finally Hunting Wolf turned away. His men were already on their ponies, waiting.

Dusk had begun to creep over the land when the war party rode away from there.

* * *

The knot was impossible to loosen, but Pritchard discovered that his teeth were making good headway on the thongs themselves, and he redoubled his efforts. Slowly his gnawing paid off, and he had almost severed the straps when suddenly a shadowy figure appeared in the door. Pritchard had barely enough time to bury his hands in his lap and hope that this dark stranger had not seen his feeble efforts at escape.

The firelight beyond completely washed away any features on the man's face. It was only when he spoke that Pritchard realized it was the young man with the scarred cheek.

"I bring you food, and water to drink," Swift Running Antelope said.

Pritchard was famished, and his mouth dry and foul-tasting from his efforts on the thongs. "That's most kind of you."

He placed a woven mat upon Pritchard's lap, and immediately the wonderful aroma of roasted elk meat set his mouth to watering. He awkwardly took the gourd of water in his bound hands and drank deeply, almost emptying it. Setting it aside, he gingerly picked at the hot meat, taking it up by his fingertips. The hot juices ran down his chin, but he did not care. He suspected this must have been a little how Buffalo Pony had felt when finally they had supplied the tyke with food he could eat.

"Thank you so much," Pritchard said between bites. "I have had nothing to eat since this morning."

"Food good?"

"Delicious!" Pritchard worked at the meat as Swift Running Antelope stood watching from the deep shadows inside the tipi. The reverend wiped his chin with his shirtsleeve and asked, "Have Mr. Carson and your chief returned yet?"

"No, they not come back."

"Maybe in the morning," Pritchard allowed hopefully. He finished the meat and reached for what was left of the water. Bringing the drinking gourd to his mouth, he happened to look out the door, and saw that the three men by the fire had returned. "Who are those men?" he asked. "They have been watching me and this tipi all afternoon, and now it is night and they still stare. They do not appear to be happy, or friendly."

Swift Running Antelope glanced out at the men and said, "There are some in the village who say that no white man can be believed. They call you Snake Tongue, and stir the people against you. But Laughing Water Woman has commanded the people that they must not bring harm to you until Hunting Wolf returns and we hear his words."

"Laughing Water Woman has ordered that?" Pritchard was somewhat surprised. He had heard that many Indian tribes were matrilineal, but he had always thought that simply meant the descendants within that tribe were reckoned from the mother's line, not the father's. He had just assumed that the men still gave the orders. After all, the chief was always a man—so far as he was aware. "Do the women rule here?"

"Rule?" Swift Running Antelope did not seem to understand the question.

"Give the orders. Are chiefs."

"No!" There was a note of indignation in his voice,

and Pritchard feared that inadvertently he had offended the young man.

"No one rules, but the elders and the people rule," Swift Running Antelope said flatly.

"Sounds very democratic. Then what is Hunting Wolf's job?"

"Hunting Wolf is chief."

"He rules?"

"Hunting Wolf is strong warrior. He leads. What is it you ask?"

Pritchard shook his head. Now he was confused. "Never mind. I see there is much I do not understand about the Indian. I was only noting that Laughing Water Woman appears to be a woman of some influence among your people."

"She has much wisdom. She is mother of chief."

"Ah, so that is it."

Swift Running Antelope collected the empty gourd and mat and started out the door. He paused, looking across at the men by the campfire and then back at Pritchard. "Do not worry about those men. You will be safe tonight."

"I'd feel a whole lot safer if my hands were not tied."

Swift Running Antelope made no reply, but stepped outside and was gone.

"Thank you very much," Pritchard said softly to himself. "Well, the Lord helps those who help themselves." With renewed energy he went back to gnawing at the leather straps, and in a few more minutes he was free of them. Shaking the thongs off and flinging them aside, he crawled to the door and cautiously peeked outside. It was still early enough that many villagers were out and moving between the campfires or sitting and chatting with friends. It was men mostly, but some women, and even a few children were yet out and about. Pritchard guessed the time to be close to nine or ten. How late these Indians stay up was anyone's guess, but they were not city dwellers. Pritchard imagined that folks living close to nature would likely follow the sun, and that soon the village would be quiet and asleep.

He sat back to try to develop a plan. Escape would not be easy in a camp full of people and dogs. Covering his trail would be even harder, for he was not a man skilled in woodcraft. But his biggest concern was what he would do once he *did* get away. He had no weapons, no idea where he was, or in which direction lay the Oregon-bound travelers whom he hoped to catch up with. He remembered his pack mules. Everything he had brought along to see him through this journey was on those mules. Even his coat!

He crawled to the back of the tipi and lifted up an edge, peering beneath it. There were only more tipis and campfires. It seemed that this particular lodge in which he was being held was more or less central to the camp. No doubt chosen for just that reason. Pritchard recalled now that other than the buffalo robe upon the floor, the place had been empty. Had it been abandoned? Where was the owner? It seemed odd that the tribe would go to the effort to erect a tipi with no intention of inhabiting it.

Now that his fetters had been removed and freeing himself was no longer the overpowering concern it had been, Reverend Pritchard began to see details of his plan that he had previously missed.

He was beginning to question the wisdom of escape in this hostile wilderness. Suddenly, what had been clear was murky. He knelt upon the buffalo robe to pray, but no soft voice spoke to him telling him what to do next. He found no comfort in what usually was a very comforting activity. It only made him more weary, and he lay upon the buffalo robe to think. Through the smoke hole overhead Orion's belt cut across a corner of his view. The stars were like glistening ice crystals in the clear mountain air. Just to look at them made Pritchard shiver, and he pulled a corner of the robe over him and closed his eyes to work upon his dilemma without distraction. . . .

A noise startled him and his eyes snapped open. He knew enough to remain absolutely still, listening. Somehow the sky overhead was all different from what he remembered. The stars had shifted. Orion was no longer visible. Then he understood. He had fallen asleep. How many hours had elapsed? What had awakened him?

Listening, he heard nothing now but the soft sighing of the wind through the village. Even the dogs were quiet. There was the far-off yipping of a coyote, and closer, the ghostly hoot of an owl, and that was all. Pritchard shifted his view toward the door flap, which was closed. He did not remember anyone coming by to close it, and reckoned that it had been done while he had been asleep. . . . Perhaps someone had even been looking in on him. That thought sent a shiver through him.

Then a sound softly reached his ear. He stiffened. It had come from nearby, very nearby, from behind him in the blackness *inside* the tipi!

Like a child imagining monsters beneath his bed,
Pritchard lay there stiff as an icicle, ears straining,
his breathing all but stopped. What was it he had
heard? Was it only his imagination? No! There it
was again. Something like breathing, only much
softer and more widely spaced, as if whatever was
lurking in the blackness was straining to make no
noise.

His fist tightened upon the buffalo robe, which he
still clutched about himself, as he listened. Whatever it was, it was to his left. To his untrained ear it
sounded as if the guarded breathing was nearer the
edge of the tipi than himself. As if someone had just
crawled in beneath the skirt of the tipi and was only
waiting. Waiting for what? For his eyes to adjust to
the deeper darkness inside than out? Or was he as-
sessing his victim, and even now on the verge of
striking? Pritchard could stand it no longer, and in
a sudden whirl of motion he flung off the robe and
leaped to his feet.

At the same instant something sprang at him
from out of the darkness. It was man-shaped, and
in the faint starlight through the smoke hole he
caught a glimpse of glinting steel slashing through
the air, striking down at him. Instinctively, Reverend Pritchard flinched aside and shot out a hand.
More by chance than design, he managed to catch
the man's wrist in mid-flight. In that instant he saw
the scowling face of an Indian glaring beyond the
knife.

Then the momentum of the strike carried both
men back against the closed door flap. The skin covering parted beneath their weight and they tumbled

outside, rolling across the ground between the dark tipis filled with their sleeping inhabitants. In the midst of the confusion, Pritchard somehow managed to keep one thought uppermost in his head. He must not allow his grip to weaken. Above all else, he must not permit the knife hand to wrench free of his grasp.

Wheeling and thrashing side to side, the Indian fought like a wildcat trying to break Pritchard's grip, all the while pummeling Pritchard with his left hand as his knee jerked violently, seeking a vulnerable spot. Pritchard had all he could do just to hold on. He was not a young man anymore, and he felt his strength draining quickly. In spite of that, he managed to draw his knees up just enough to protect his groin and gut, but that was about all.

They rolled across the shadowy ground until finally his attacker had gained the upper hand. With the Indian's weight now behind the knife, he was rapidly overpowering Pritchard's weakening arms. The preacher gritted his teeth and held on for dear life. His breathing had become labored, bursting from his lungs in short, ragged gasps.

Then there came the sounds of footsteps nearby, and hope momentarily swelled within the flagging preacher. But even that last glimmer of help vanished when a second pair of hands suddenly grabbed his wrist and wrenched his hold away from his attacker.

He was helpless to stop it, held there by two men. A third warrior suddenly appeared from the darkness. He fell upon Pritchard and crushed a knee into his arm while at the same time clamping a hand over his mouth. Pritchard could do absolutely nothing now to defend himself. All he could do was watch with wide-eyed terror as the knife arced upward, then plunged toward his breast.

Chapter Nine

A cry ripped through the night air, shattering the silence in the sleeping village. Startled by its sound, the man with the knife hesitated, glancing up. At that same moment something from out of the darkness took flight, and the next instant a warrior slammed into the man with the knife and knocked him off the preacher. The two men struck the ground hard, and at once this newcomer wrenched the knife away and scrambled atop Pritchard's assailant, levering the man's arm up between his shoulder blades. The two who held Pritchard pinned to the ground suddenly released him and tried to scurry away. But the war whoop had roused the sleeping village, and now people were pouring out of the lodges.

The villains had nowhere to run as people gathered around. Pritchard pushed himself up and sat there, stunned. It had all happened so quickly that barely thirty seconds had passed from the instant he had confronted the intruder in his tipi until this very moment. In a daze he looked up at the Shoshonis standing above him, some nearly naked, others hugging buffalo robes about their shoulders, all looking faintly dazed themselves, having just been pulled from sleep by that bloodcurdling cry. . . .

Pritchard shot a glance back to where the two men had fought their brief struggle. It turned out to be Swift Running Antelope who was straddling his attacker. It was the young warrior who had saved him. There was much talk among the people, none of which he understood. Swift Running Antelope released the man and stood just as several older men arrived and began questioning him. They all turned and frowned at the three men who had attacked Pritchard.

Two men grabbed Pritchard's arms, hauled him to his feet, and stood him with the others. "What is happening?" he asked.

Swift Running Antelope glanced his way. "Later," he said, and turned back to the elders. Then the crowd parted and Laughing Water Woman strode into their midst. She looked somehow older than Pritchard remembered, clutching a robe about herself, and like most everyone else, barefooted and sleepy-eyed. She listened as Swift Running Antelope told what had happened, glancing occasionally at the three men. When he finished, Laughing Water Woman's dark stare settled heavily upon Pritchard. At her command the two warriors holding his arms took him to the tipi and shoved him through the door.

From the dark confines inside the skin lodge Pritchard listened to their voices. Although the words were all gibberish, the tone was plainly that of an argument heating up. In a moment a half-dozen or more men were clamoring to be heard. All at once Laughing Water Woman's voice rang out, and suddenly there was silence. Mumbling among themselves, the spectators went back to their lodges, and in a few minutes the village was quiet. Pritchard sat in the dark shivering, not from the cold, but from the close brush with death.

Then a man spoke outside as a new set of guards took their station. Pritchard recognized Swift Running Antelope's voice. The warrior bent through the door and stood there staring down at him.

"You are all right?"

"Yes. Thanks to you they did not injure me."

"I thought this might happen when you pointed them out to me. Lame Foot and Soaring Eagle are—" He halted, groping for a word.

"Troublemakers?"

"Yes. As you say. The third man with them, Far Thunder, is weak in spirit and is easily led into trouble."

"We too have men like that. Unfortunately, more so than not," Pritchard replied. "You were watching then?"

The young man nodded his head.

"I must assume that you believe me. Otherwise why should you care what happens?"

"Believe? This I cannot say yet, not until Hunting Wolf returns. But I see in you a man who cares deeply for the little one. A man like that does not kill women and children."

Pritchard was gratified to hear that, although a firm *yes* was what he really needed from the man and these people. "What was said out there?"

"Soaring Eagle told Grandmother that you were trying to escape."

"But that is not true."

Swift Running Antelope did not speak at once. Pritchard would have liked to have better seen his face, to read what the man was thinking. "Your hands are no longer bound," he pointed out. "Soaring Eagle says that proves you were trying to escape."

Sheepishly Pritchard looked at his hands, then gave the warrior a wry smile. "It is true. I did free myself with the plan of escaping." He shrugged and looked away, embarrassed to admit his own ineptitude in a matter as important as fleeing from there. "But I fell asleep."

The Indian laughed softly. "I believe this, for I saw the way you *escaped*, tumbling from the lodge with Soaring Eagle on top of you." His voice turned serious. "Behind the lodge I discovered the place where Soaring Eagle entered. You were lucky. He would have killed you quietly in your sleep if you had not awakened."

"Lucky? My guardian angel was standing watch over me, I am sure of it."

"Guardian angel? Ah, the spirit your people worship. I have heard of such things among white men while trading with them."

"Laughing Water Woman does not believe me, does she?"

"She grieves for the daughters and grandchildren she has lost. Like all the people, she waits for word from Hunting Wolf."

Again, it all came down to that. What was Hunting Wolf going to tell them when he returned? If he could not be convinced of their innocence, then Pritchard was doomed. And if that was to be the case, then Pritchard feared that Kit Carson was already dead. The thought made him shudder. This was not at all what he had imagined it would be like when he had planned to come west and minister to these children of the wilderness. But then what *had* he thought? That they would have accepted him unquestioningly? Opened their arms to him and marched happily into Sunday services? That coming into these wild lands would not be accompanied by hardships? Perhaps more hardships than rewards? Was he really cut out for this line of work after all?

"I suppose you will want to tie my hands again," he said. He was too weary and depressed to fight it anymore.

"Would you struggle to free them again if I did?"

"No. No more. Not tonight. I shall wait for Mr. Carson and Hunting Wolf to return and pray that your chief will have seen the truth in what we have already told him."

"Then I will not tie you up tonight."

"You won't?"

"If you are a man of true words, you will be here in the morning. If not, I will hunt you down and cut out your tongue. Laughing Water Woman has told the guard to remain until morning. Soaring Eagle and his friends will not trouble you again. Tomorrow they will stand before the elders, and perhaps be punished for what they tried here tonight."

A question had been weighing on Pritchard's mind ever since the previous day when the warrior had tried to suffocate little Buffalo Pony, and no one had seemed to mind. The preacher asked Swift Running Antelope about it now.

The young warrior only laughed and said, "Many Arrows was not harming the child. It is the Shoshoni way."

"I don't understand."

"It is not the way of our people to allow the cry of a baby. In times of battle that could reveal the hiding places of the child, or his people."

"Mr. Carson said something about Indian babies being taught not to cry."

"He speaks true words. When the baby cries, his mother pinches the nose and holds a hand over the mouth. He cannot breathe, and soon learns that the crying brings much discomfort. There are many little ones in the village, Pritchard, but if you listen you will not hear them cry."

"You are right. I have not heard an infant's cry since arriving. But I have heard much laughter."

Swift Running Antelope merely smiled, as if resting his case.

"I fear that I have been foolish," Pritchard said. "There is so much I need to learn."

"Why?"

"Why? Well, because I want to help. To minister to the Indians of the Far West."

Swift Running Antelope cocked his head slightly to the right, as if trying to make sense out of that.

Pritchard heard something outside. "What is that?"

Swift Running Antelope listened a moment. "Rider comes in."

"At this hour?"

Concern suddenly narrowed the Shoshoni's eyes. The warrior stepped outside and Pritchard followed him. Others had heard the sounds of approaching hoofbeats too, and once again sleepy-eyed Indians stumbled out of their tipis. Pritchard followed Swift Running Antelope through the maze of lodges to the edge of the village, where a lone figure was swiftly coming in from the east. There was a faint tint of color in the horizon that signaled the approaching dawn. Three or four other men showed up, giving Pritchard a stare, but saying nothing about him being there. They just assumed he was with Swift Running Antelope and left it at that.

"Do you know who it is?" Pritchard asked.

"Yes. It is Broken Hoof. He must be bringing word from Hunting Wolf."

Pritchard felt his heart climb into his throat. Just a few minutes ago the moment of reckoning seemed distant. Now suddenly it was upon him. He had a growing fear that whatever news this lone warrior was bringing, it was almost certainly going to change his present conditions . . . one way or the other. And he wasn't all that sure his predicament was about to improve.

Glancing around, he saw that to the north there were hardly any people. The south end of the village seemed to have attracted them all. Perhaps here was a possible avenue of escape. He still had a few moments. No one would notice him slipping away now that the village's attention was riveted upon this incoming rider.

He took a step backward. Then another. The crowd was moving away from him, and with them Swift Running Antelope. Pritchard took a third step, and then suddenly stopped. Had he not given his word to Swift Running Antelope that he would not try to escape? Did his word hold no value? Was it so easily set aside now, when an opportunity was open to him? Ruefully, Pritchard realized that two of his constant companions, trust and integrity, were rearing their heads in defiance again. How could he ever hope to escape when such things bound him tighter than the Indian's leather thongs had bound his wrists. Knowing he could never fight them, he slumped his shoulders, dropped his head, and like a lamb being led to the slaughter, moved with the crowd toward the rider already reining to a stop among the anxious people.

There were about two minutes of rapid-fire questions and answers, and then the men scattered, hurrying off to their lodges. The rider, escorted by some of the men, started across the village, heading for Laughing Water Woman's lodge. Swift Running Antelope started away too, but just then spied Pritchard standing there and came over.

"What is the news?" the preacher asked cautiously, not certain he was ready to hear the answer. There was much commotion in the village as men scurried about and dogs, sensing the excitement, began to bark. Curious faces of women appeared in the door flaps of several of the tipis as their men returned to tell them of the rider's message.

"Broken Hoof brings word that it is as you and Carson told it."

Relief swept over Pritchard.

"The bodies were found. It was Blackfeet who killed them. Hunting Wolf is riding to do battle with our enemy. He is calling for warriors to join with him."

"And what of Mr. Carson?"

"Hunting Wolf did not speak of him. But Hunting Wolf says you are to be released and not harmed. You are to be an honored guest of the village."

"A guest? But isn't Mr. Carson coming back for me? I must catch up with my friends. I can't remain here."

"Then you can go."

"Go? By myself? How shall I ever find them?"

"This we will talk about later, when the warriors return." Swift Running Antelope left him standing there, and angled across the ground toward his lodge.

"But I can't wait that long!" Pritchard called after him. Suddenly he was alone—alone in the middle of a village of Indians scurrying about preparing for war. He returned to his tipi, but stood outside it watching the horses being brought from the corral and saddled while men filled their quivers with arrows, slung bows across their shoulders, scooped little children up into their arms, and hugged wives.

As the new day brightened to the east, more than two dozen warriors prepared to leave. Then Pritchard spied Swift Running Antelope coming toward him with a pretty woman walking along at his side. She appeared to be no older than fifteen or sixteen, and she was very pregnant. Her hair hung in long braids down her back, and swung from side to side as she hurried to keep up with Swift Running Antelope.

"Pritchard. I go now with the men to fight the Blackfeet."

"I wish you Godspeed. I am sorry you must leave. I am confused as to what is to happen to me, and you are the only one with whom I can speak."

"That is why I come to you now. This is my wife." He spoke her name quickly in the Shoshoni language, then translated it for him. "In your tongue she is called Green Hummingbird."

"Ma'am," he said, nodding. He would have tipped his hat had he been wearing one.

"She speaks the tongue of the white man. I teach," he said, puffing up his chest briefly. "She speak not good like me, but she will help you until I return."

Green Hummingbird smiled at him, showing a row of uneven teeth. "I help you," she said eagerly.

"Thank you, Green Hummingbird," he replied, trying to sound grateful, but fretting even more over whether or not he was ever going to see his friends again. "Has there been anything said of Mr. Carson?" he asked Swift Running Antelope. "Any word at all?"

The warrior shook his head. "Broken Hoof say only that the white man ride away to warn friends, and to fight Blackfeet."

"Fight the Blackfeet?" Pritchard struggled against a sudden wave of despair. "If Mr. Carson goes to war he might be killed. And if that were to happen . . ." He looked around himself at the tipis and the half-wild people about. He squelched a shudder and refused to consider his fate should the mountain man be unable to return for him.

Kit Carson would return. He must return!

Swift Running Antelope gave his wife a brief hug. There was no kissing, no overt passion in his leaving. Merely a few words that Pritchard did not understand, and then the warrior turned and walked to the waiting men. He did not look back at his wife, and it was plain that Green Hummingbird did not expect him to do so. The warriors mounted up and rode away.

When they had gone, the village went back to its regular morning routine—at least Pritchard assumed it was a normal routine. He had no way of knowing for certain, of course, but there was a tension in the air that somehow had been lacking the previous day when he'd arrived. Perhaps the children did not laugh as loudly, or the women smile as freely.

Whatever it was, Pritchard felt it. He felt it just as surely as if these had been his own people, the cultured folks of the East whom he had known all his life. He remembered the taste and texture of this same tension years ago when the young men had gone off the fight the British in 1812. And before that, when he had been but a boy and his father and uncles had marched off to battle King George's Redcoats for independence.

Standing there, Green Hummingbird smiled at him a little uncertainly.

Lamely, he smiled back.

Chapter Ten

Suddenly, he had complete freedom to roam the village. Other than the stares he received from the curious and the cautious, no one tried to stop William Pritchard from going anywhere he wanted.

After Green Hummingbird had gone back to her lodge, Pritchard strolled toward the corral at the far end of the village. His horse and mules were there, his saddle resting off to one side along with the packs that contained all his belongings. He was surprised to discover that they had not been molested. Everything was exactly as he had left it.

There were two guards nearby, watching over the animals. They stopped talking and grinned at him as he approached.

Pritchard smiled in return. "Hello," he said, hoping to hear a word in English in reply. But they obviously did not understand him. They spoke back in

Shoshoni. It was amiable, but utterly unintelligible to Pritchard. He lingered by the brush corral, watching his animals nip the sparse grass, weighing his chances of striking out on his own. He was rapidly despairing of ever seeing Kit Carson again.

Could he make it on his own?

Perhaps.

He had a pistol and a rifle. He had observed the caution that Kit Carson, and Harold Cassin before him, had used while crossing Indian territory. He could read the compass points from the sun as well as any man. And a caravan of a dozen wagons, horses, oxen, and cows would leave behind wide, deep tracks. He'd seen them plainly enough at the start of their trip. Was there any why reason he could not find them once again and then easily follow them? The wagons and cattle would leave a clear trail all the way to Oregon for him to follow. In fact, all he had to do was follow the tracks left that morning by the Shoshoni and he would find Spalding and the others. He was certain of it.

Pritchard walked back into the village, determined to make a try of it on his own. He told himself that he was only anxious to be on his way . . . to his calling . . . his mission. But a small voice at the back of his brain was whispering something else to him. Was he really anxious to go to the Indians in Oregon? Or was it that he wanted to flee from these poor, uncivilized people? Then he stopped and had to ask himself a question. Were the people he was going to any different from these? Most likely not, he had to admit. If these folks frightened him, then what was he doing out here in the first place? What sort of missionary was he anyway?

Just then something caught the corner of his eye. Instinctively he stopped and jerked back as a small brown projectile whizzed past his head and thumped onto the ground a few feet away. He heard a rush of feet, and when he turned, three boys skidded to a halt and stared at him, uncertain if it was safe to proceed. Pritchard looked back as a leather ball rolled to a stop a few feet away. He grinned and retrieved the ball.

The boys watched him scoop it up, and appeared concerned that he was going to keep it. But their expression turned to delight as Pritchard wound up and threw the ball high into the air toward the center of the village. The boys scurried about, hands reaching for the sky as the leather ball completed its arc and started down. One of them managed to get beneath it, and expertly snatched it from the air as it whirled toward the ground. The boys laughed and gave forth a cry that might have been akin to a cheer in another place and another time. Then the dark-haired fellow who had caught it turned to Pritchard and said something, and they all scampered off.

Of course Pritchard did not understand a word of it, but the meaning was clear enough. If this had been Virginia instead of the wilderness mountains west of the Green River, he imagined the parting remark might have been along the lines of, "Thanks, mister."

Pritchard thought it remarkable that way out here in this savage wilderness, boys were pretty much the same as the boys he'd known back East. He grinned again and shook his head as he resumed his march to the tipi for his hat. He knew he had to be leaving soon, while there was still a full day's worth of daylight ahead of him.

"Pritchard."

Startled at the sound of his name, he hauled himself around. It was Green Hummingbird hailing him from the door of a tipi. It took a moment before he realized that the tipi was that of Laughing Water Woman.

"Yes?" he asked, strolling over to where she was standing.

"Grandmother . . . " Green Hummingbird grasped for a word. "Talk to you."

"She wishes to speak with me?"

The young woman nodded her head and stepped aside to let him enter the tipi. It was a larger place than the one he'd been kept in, but in most respects very similar. There was a skirt of skins that formed a circle around the inside walls of the lodge. Behind these he could see packs of skins, baskets, blankets, and other odds and ends poking out here and there. Most of it he could not identify. In the center burned a small fire. Its smoke trailed straight up and out the open flap at the pinnacle of the tipi. Upon the coals sat an iron pot, most likely acquired in trade with white trappers. The floor was covered with buffalo skins, and to the left sat a framework of willow branches that appeared to be a weaver's frame. There were two doeskin dresses folded neatly nearby, and a couple of woven mats on which sat a drinking gourd and a clay bowl filled with something that looked like stew, or gruel. He could not be certain in the poor light inside. The sight of it reminded him how hungry he was.

To the right was a sleeping pallet padded with skins and blankets, and upon this lay Laughing Water Woman, her back propped up against a woven backrest. She wore a fringed dress and had a white and green point blanket pulled up over her shoulders. She looked old and frail, but upon closer examination Pritchard decided that the woman was not really all that old. Perhaps no more that fifty years of age; younger than he! She just *looked* old. Her skin was pallid, her eyes runny, drooping with a sickly yellowish cast to them. She held a hand against her jaw, pressing something that looked like a clump of steaming moss to it. Nearby, a bowl of smoldering sticks filled the tipi with a thick, hazy smoke that stung Pritchard's eyes.

"Hello," he said softly. Green Hummingbird translated. Laughing Water Woman nodded briefly, and indicated a leather pillow decorated in polished porcupine quills. Pritchard lowered himself to it, finding it quite comfortable.

The older woman spoke slowly, carefully, wincing occasionally.

"Grandmother say, much grateful that Pritchard help the people, and much sad because grandchildren and daughters are no more. But happy you saved Buffalo Pony."

"Tell Laughing Water Woman I am honored to be able to have been of service to your people. I only wish I could have prevented the tragedy in the first place. But there is Mr. Carson to thank as well. He was the one who found them."

She had some trouble grasping all of that, but managed to get a handle on most of it and make the gist of what Pritchard had said clear to Grandmother. When Laughing Water Woman spoke, her long, bony finger lifted and pointed first this way, then that.

"Men who attack last night stand before elders today. They will be banished from village for two winters," Green Hummingbird translated.

Pritchard merely nodded. He could not possibly comment on Shoshoni justice, not understanding it. Banishment in their culture was perhaps the same as a jail sentence in his. Perhaps worse. He had no way of knowing. "I am certain that your elders will do what is right."

Laughing Water Woman spoke to the young woman. Green Hummingbird said, "Grandmother say you eat little. You hungry now. She give you food." The young woman indicated the gourd and bowl.

"For me?"

She nodded.

He was touched by the gesture. But uncertain. "What is it?" he asked, trying to sound merely curious.

"Food," she reiterated, as if it was obvious.

Pritchard considered pressing further to discover the contents of this *food*, but didn't think he would learn too much. Nor was he certain he wanted to. He was hungry, and the likelihood of him finding plentiful food these next few days while he searched for Kit Carson was questionable at best. His spirit was suddenly heavy with concern for the trapper's safety. He'd almost forgotten that Kit Carson was risking a fight with murdering Blackfeet in order to warn the Oregon-bound travelers. He put that thought out of his head and with both women look-

ing on, picked up the bowl, which was quite warm
Since no utensils were provided, Pritchard figured it
was customary to use one's fingers.

He fished up a piece of meat and tasted it. It was
elk! That gave him a bit more confidence, and he ate
some more. "This is good," he told Green Hummingbird. She smiled, pleased that he liked it.
Pritchard found that the stew contained wild
onions, turnips, bits of a white, spicy root he could
not identify, and what appeared to be crushed
berries. He thought it could use a bit of salt and pep-
per, but beyond that, the stew was delightfully palat-
able. He finished it off in short order, licking his
fingers clean and washing it down with a long drink
of water.

When he had put the gourd back alongside the
empty bowl and thanked them both, he added,
"Now, might I ask you a question, Laughing Water
Woman?"

Green Hummingbird translated.

She nodded her head.

"You appear to be in much pain. Swift Running
Antelope told me you suffer from the yellow poison.
I wonder if you would permit me to help you."

"Grandmother says the medicine man has given
her a poultice and has burned sage and cedar."
Green Hummingbird pointed to the smoldering pot
at Grandmother's side.

"Has the treatment relieved the pain?" he asked.

He saw the disappointment in Green Hummingbird's eyes. "No, but it will help soon, the medicine
man says. The spirits have to be encouraged. Ninnimbe is in hiding, and must be found and driven
from our lands before Grandmother is well again."

Ninnimbe? Pritchard had heard that name before.
Then he remembered. The previous night when
Laughing Water Woman and Swift Running Antelope had visited him in the tipi. "What if he is not
found?"

She frowned deeply and lowered her voice when
she spoke, even though the older woman obviously
did not understand a word of English. "The yellow
poison will steal her spirit and carry it away."

"I see. You know, there may be something I can do
to help. I am a trained physician. If only she will
permit me to examine her."

Green Hummingbird related this, and received a
firm shake of the old woman's head in reply.

"Well, in any event I will say a prayer for her. This
she cannot prevent me from doing." He stood and
told them good-bye, saying that he was planning to
depart shortly and follow the warriors in hopes of
eventually catching up with Mr. Carson and his
friends.

He left the tipi with a new heaviness of heart.
These people had showed him friendship, and he
only wished to return friendship. But their tradi-
tions, their *superstitions*, would not permit it, and
because of that, the old woman would likely die of
an infection Pritchard was certain he could remedy!

"Ninnimbe!" he said aloud, crossing to the tipi
and stepping inside just long enough to grab up his
tall hat. Back at the corral he told the guards he was
taking his animals and leaving. They did not understand his words, but his intentions were clear and
no one made any attempt to stop him.

It took a half an hour to repack the two mules and
saddle his horse. His activities drew a small crowd

of curious onlookers. Among them were the three boys who had been playing catch with the leather ball. They had since put the ball away in favor of long war lances with wickedly sharp iron tips eight inches long. Pritchard had observed them hurling these spears at a leather sack, vaguely in the shape of a man and stuffed with grass, just a few minutes before they had wandered over to see what he was up to.

Pritchard tried to ignore the curious faces and concentrate on his plans. He was certain he could follow the war party's tracks well enough. His only concern was if he would find Kit Carson and the others at the end of his quest. And more importantly, would he find them alive?

The boys must have gotten bored watching him. After a few minutes of it they grabbed up their war lances, let loose with a shrill mock war cry, and darted away to pincushion the stuffed target some more.

Pritchard gave a wry smile. Oh, to be a boy once again, without a care in the world, playing ball and making pretend war. How like his own son were these three. Only difference was, back then the target at the far end of his son's squirrel gun had been pretend Indians. His smile widened into a full-blown grin. And perhaps that stuffed sack of grass was a pretend white man.

He drew the ropes tight and gave them a final snap to test them. He was all ready to go. As he looked around at the people and the village, he felt a strange resistance to his plans now. His view lingered a moment upon Laughing Water Woman's tipi. A small voice in his head seemed to be urging him to remain there.

Defiantly, he shrugged it off.

"I'm leaving, and that is all there is to it!" he declared to himself, and stuck his foot into the stirrup of his saddle.

From beyond one of the tipis came a sudden wail. It was not the playful mock war cries of boys pretending to be men in battle that Pritchard had been hearing all along, but a startled yelp of real pain mixed with a growing panic.

The people immediately rushed toward the boy's cry for help.

Suspended there halfway between ground and saddle, Pritchard watched folks fleeing from all parts of the village, gathering someplace just beyond his view. The wail grew in a most untypical fashion for a people who rarely allowed pain to show.

Concerned, Pritchard lowered himself back to the ground and found himself trailing after the hurrying people. As he rounded a tipi, he saw that a crowd had gathered around something upon the ground. Standing off to one side were two of the boys, their eyes huge and faces draining of color, a pair of lances lying at their feet.

Where was the third boy? he wondered. The laughing fellow who had snatched the ball from the air and shouted his thanks in return?

Then a man moved aside and Pritchard spied the lad. The preacher's heart thumped and his throat constricted at the sight of the boy writhing in agony with a spear through his thigh.

121

Doug Hawkins

From the wound surged a fountain of blood. To Pritchard's trained eye that could mean only one thing!

"My God!" he breathed, rushing forward.

Chapter Eleven

Pritchard had to muscle his way through the crowd. Someone grabbed him by the arm to hold him back. He wrenched free and pushed close enough to see past one or two men to where the boy lay.

One of the men grabbed the spear's shaft and withdrew the long iron point from his leg. Trying to hold back, the boy groaned and cried out again. A woman with panic written across her face fell to his side and cradled his head upon her knees. One of the man grabbed the leg and stared at the fountain of blood. He squeezed down on it, but the flow did not subside in the least.

Pritchard listened to the anxious words sweeping through the crowd, waited to see if anyone would come forward with any medical knowledge on the matter. No one did. The boy would bleed to death in minutes if something wasn't done at once. He forced his way past the onlookers and dropped to his knees at the lad's side. Someone grabbed at him and tried to haul him away.

"Let me be!" he roared turning and glaring with eyes afire. Suddenly Green Hummingbird was there. He shot her a glance and said, "Tell them the boy is bleeding to death."

"They know. But only medicine man can help."

"What? Then where is he?"

"Calling Elk is not here. Him with the men to fight Blackfeet."

"Calling Elk?" Pritchard recalled the name. It belonged the stout man who had ridden at Hunting Wolf's side. He remembered that it had been Calling Elk who had stopped Hunting Wolf from killing them immediately. Although the preacher had not understood anything that had transpired between the Indians and Kit Carson at the time, he had gotten the distinct feeling that Calling Elk was a wise, thoughtful man. Now he understood why. "This boy cannot wait for Calling Elk to return. He will be dead in minutes if not treated at once! I can help him."

As she tried to translate that, Pritchard unbuttoned his canvas suspenders and slipped them off his shoulders. In a moment he had fashioned a tourniquet and was twisting it about the boy's thigh. But the artery was deep and he still could not apply enough pressure. He turned to a man nearby and said, "Give me your knife!"

The man stared at him.

Pritchard pointed and opened his palm.

Reluctantly, the man passed it across to him. Pritchard thrust its handle in the knotted suspenders and gave two turns. Slowly, very slowly the spurting blood receded to a slow flow. This gave Pritchard time to examine the wound. The spear had entered the upper inside thigh and gone clean through. But the volume of blood could mean only one thing.

"He has severed the femoral artery," he said to Green Hummingbird, knowing the words meant nothing to her. He was talking to himself, thinking through the emergency aloud. Was it a nick or a complete cut? The latter would almost certainly mean death if not repaired.

Suddenly a fierce face hovered before him, growling out angry words. The man pointed, clearly ordering Pritchard away from there.

Green Hummingbird said, "Rolling Thunder say only a medicine man can touch the boy now. Rolling Thunder say you must go."

"Oh, is that so?" Pritchard glared back at the man, who must have been an elder of the tribe for he had long gray hair and appeared to be giving Methuselah a run for his money.

"Well, you just tell Rolling Thunder that I *am* a medicine man. From where I come from I am called . . . I am called . . . " he stammered, trying to think fast and suddenly not able to. "I am called Elijah! And if he does not permit me to help the boy, I will call fire down from out of the sky to consume all the buffalo!"

Oh, why had he used that example? Pritchard lamented. Quickly he shot up a prayer asking God to forgive him for having borrowed so freely from one of the Old Testament prophets, imploring that these Indians would not press the matter to the point where they would call his bluff.

Green Hummingbird gave a rough translation of the threat. When he heard her say the name "Elijah," he winced and looked away. Immediately a silence fell upon the crowd, and the old man stepped cautiously back.

Pritchard drew in a huge sigh of relief and turned his attention to the wound. The boy was stiff as a tree and groaning in pain. Pritchard tried to examine the long gash, but his efforts only tortured the lad more.

"Green Hummingbird. We need to move the boy into a lodge and then someone must bring me my surgical instruments—err, my medicine bag."

He kept pressure on the tourniquet as they lifted the boy and carried him into a tipi. The boy's mother quickly prepared the sleeping pallet for him. A few moments later Green Hummingbird informed Pritchard that the mules were waiting outside. They had brought them because no one knew what a white man's medicine bag looked like. Pritchard put her hand upon the knife and told her to keep the tourniquet tight. He rushed outside, flung off the cords and canvas coverings, and found his bag of surgical instruments. Looking over the other supplies he had brought to set up practice in Oregon, he selected a small, sectioned wooden box that held half-a-dozen sealed bottles.

The tipi was overcrowded with the curious, and Pritchard ordered everyone out except Green Hummingbird, the boy's mother, and a stout fellow named Badger who might be of help if restraining the boy became necessary. After hearing the command from his translator's lips, the people grumbled and reluctantly retreated, filling the doorway instead with their faces.

"Tell them they are blocking the light."

She did, and they hesitantly gave more ground. It appeared to him that every tipi in the village was oriented so that its door faced east. At this hour of the morning the climbing sun gave Pritchard sharp, bright light to work by. He opened the sectioned box and quickly examined the labels on the bottles, selecting two of them and replacing the others.

"Have some warm water brought here," he said, unwrapping a lump of green lye soap from a piece of cheesecloth. While he waited for its arrival, Pritchard studied the label upon a bottle marked "Laudanum." It was a dilution of the drug. He eyed the child, who was no more that ten or twelve, and guessed his weight to be at around sixty pounds. Pritchard worked out a safe dosage, then broke the waxed seal and worked the cork from the bottle's neck. Using a measure from his bag, he poured out the correct amount, then gently lifting the boy's head from his mother's lap, put the drug to his lips. After a taste the boy readily took the thick, sweet liquid, and even licked his lips afterwards.

"In a few minutes the pain will stop," he reassured him.

The water came, and Pritchard rolled up his sleeves and washed his hands with the soap. But when he passed it to the husky Indian beside him, the man merely looked at it.

"Wash hands," Pritchard said rubbing his own together to demonstrate. "Yes, yes, I know, it makes no sense, but do it anyway. Please tell him."

Green Hummingbird was becoming frazzled trying to keep up with her limited English.

Pritchard went on. "I don't know if it matters or not, but I have read reports from England that a clean surgery has been found to reduce the chance of infection. No one knows why. Some think it may have something to do with Leeuwenhoek's 'Wee Beasties.' The truth to tell, the reason is anyone's guess, but if it will help in the least, then I am all for employing the technique." He looked over. Green Hummingbird was staring at him in despair. Pritchard gave a short laugh and said, "Forget all of that. Just tell him he must wash his hands like I have just done."

She managed that much. With a look of disgust, the Indian clumsily complied.

"What is the boy's name?"

Green Hummingbird glanced around the tipi as if somehow she was afraid of being overheard. She whispered, "He is called Climb-to-the-Top."

Climb-to-the-Top had become very relaxed now. This seemed to distress his mother more than his previous show of pain. Pritchard reassured her it was all right. He turned his attention to the ugly wound. Frowning, he probed the deep gash with a fingertip. The boy winced, but nothing more than that. In a few minutes Pritchard had determined the extent of the injury.

"The femoral artery feels as if it is nicked, but not severed."

"That bad?" she asked.

"That is bad, but it could have been much worse. If not repaired, the boy might lose his leg. That is, if he does not bleed to death first."

128

Green Hummingbird glanced at the mother, then back without translating Pritchard's diagnosis of the matter.

"You heal boy?"

"I will try." He opened the other bottle and set it aside. From his surgery kit he removed a scalpel, tweezers, a needle, and suturing thread. "Tell Badger to hold the boy's leg."

Pritchard examined his scalpel in the light through the doorway. Before leaving the States he had carefully prepared all his surgical instruments, and now the fine edge of the cutting tool gleamed in the sunlight. He plunged the tool into the open bottle of alcohol. Every eye watched warily as he put the blade to the boy's leg. They all seemed to be holding their breaths—himself included.

Then a shadow fell across them. Pritchard looked up. Laughing Water Woman was standing in the doorway peering down at him. Her eyes moved toward the scalpel, then to the boy's face. Climb-to-the-Top appeared serenely unconcerned now. Wordlessly, she stepped inside the tipi and stood against the inner curtain, out of their way.

One more pair of eyes wasn't going to matter now, and putting them all out of his mind, he made an incision to open the skin so that he had more room to work.

"You know," he said, his attention focused upon the delicate task at hand, "it was not so long ago that the only way to treat a severed artery was to cauterize it. But surgery has made great leaps in this area, thanks to a Frenchman named Ambroise Paré who developed the technique of ligation. Fortunately, I do not have to ligate this artery as it is not completely severed. What I am attempting here is a procedure that is quite extraordinary and exacting. I have read of the technique only."

Green Hummingbird merely listened and watched. She had given up on trying to follow his ramblings as he worked at the wound. He clamped the artery with a pair of locking tweezers, and with a second pair of tweezers he was manipulating the artery and making precise stitches. Slowly, deftly, he repaired the section of the thick blood vessel that had been sliced by the spear.

Throughout the whole procedure Laughing Water Woman watched silently, not uttering a word.

Satisfied with the job, Pritchard closed the wound and expertly stitched the skin back together. He had lost track of the time, but when he finally finished the surgery, the sun no longer showed through the doorway.

As quietly as she had arrived, Laughing Water Woman left. Not a single word had been uttered the whole time.

The boy came through the surgery with flying colors, still enjoying the fuzzy-headedness of the laudanum. That would pass shortly, and when it did, Climb-to-the-Top was in for a lot of pain. Pritchard finished off his handiwork with a medicinal salve from his "medicine bag," and wrapped the wound in a gauze bandage.

"I will look in on him later," he told the boy's mother.

When he and Green Hummingbird stepped outside, she asked, "You not leave now?"

William Pritchard frowned. "I want to go. I very badly wish to rejoin my friends. But I feel I ought to remain here to watch the boy, at least through the day. I think all will be right with the lad, but there is still the concern of infection."

Suddenly Green Hummingbird winced, and she placed a hand upon her swollen belly.

"Are you all right?" he asked her.

She smiled and nodded. "I all right. I go to lodge now."

"Yes, by all means. You have been of immense help to me, Green Hummingbird, and you look exhausted. Thank you very much."

He watched the young girl waddle away in the manner of women who are well along in their pregnancy. Pritchard looked at his hands, at the bloodstains upon the turned-up cuffs of his shirt, and started toward the stream to wash up. As he was passing the open door of a nearby tipi he happened to glance in and see a naked baby upon a buffalo skin rug, laughing and kicking his chubby legs at the air.

"Little Chief!" he declared. He was delighted to see the infant well and happy. He stopped and peered inside. A young woman of about twenty years was sitting upon the ground with her legs tucked up beneath her, weaving thin willow branches into a mat or a basket of some sort. Like all the women he had seen in the village so far, this one wore her black hair in two long braids, each encased in a band of leather, laces, and some bits of bone worked into a design. She wore a leather dress that had seen better days, with long fringe and a small amount of beadwork across its shoulders. Asleep in a cradleboard at one side of the tipi was a second baby. Pritchard's sudden appearance startled her.

131

"Hello," he said, smiling.

There was a momentary look of concern upon her face, but it passed quickly. Pritchard's reputation had obviously preceded him. By now, he reckoned, the entire village knew of his efforts to save the boy.

"How is the little one doing?"

The woman tilted her head to one side. She did not understand a word. She set her woodcraft down upon her lap and looked at him with dark brown eyes that were wide and attentive.

"Little Chief, that's what we called him before we knew his name."

She said something in reply, and they both smiled at their shared lack of understanding.

"May I hold him?" he asked.

She blinked.

He folded his arms in a gesture of cradling a baby to himself.

The woman nodded.

Pritchard ducked inside the tipi and gently lifted the infant. He cradled him in his arms a few moments, making baby-sounds and tickling Buffalo Pony's chin. The baby laughed. Pritchard smiled, and his fingers nearly encircling the little fellow's chest as he held him out at arm's length, he said, "You look much happier now than the first time we met."

Buffalo Pony cooed and kicked his legs.

Pritchard grinned.

Then the baby boy peed on him.

Startled, he could do nothing but watch as his shirt grew a wide warm wet spot in the middle.

The woman giggled, turning her face away to hide her laughter behind her hand.

"Thank you, thank you very much for that, young man," Pritchard said, setting the baby back on the skin and looking down at himself.

Wiping a tear from the corner of her eye, the woman fought to refrain from grinning too widely.

Pritchard plucked at his shirt, lifting the warm, wet material away from his chest. "Well, I was on my way to wash up. It looks as if the matter has just become doubly urgent." Taking up his medical bag, he gave her a small wave.

She waved back, still holding back a smile as he retreated from the tipi and turned his steps quickly toward the stream beyond the village.

Chapter Twelve

Kit Carson hunkered down alongside the trail to study the tracks. Running a finger around the edges of one of the imprints, he plucked out a small branch from the crushed earth and turned it toward the sunlight coming through the tall pine trees. A bit of the bark had been peeled back. The wood beneath it was green and still moist. He walked along the trace a little farther and found horse manure, still warm. All along the trail the tracks of unshod ponies trampled the deep wheel ruts that the heavily laden, ox-drawn wagons had left behind.

The Blackfeet were only an hour ahead of him now, maybe less. The pilgrims, perhaps half a day beyond. The Indians were closing in on McKay and his party, and Kit on the Indians. Unencumbered by Reverend Pritchard and his mules, which had made travel slow going at best, Kit had ridden hard since leaving the Shoshonis the evening before. By pushing himself and his horse, he had made up much of his lost time.

The Blackfeet had been steadily gaining on McKay too, but they were doing so at a pace calculated to reserve their strength for the battle to come. They did not suffer from the same urgency that had driven Kit for almost twenty straight hours.

Gathering up his reins, Kit leaped back onto his horse and pushed on. In a few minutes he swung off the trail he had been following and made a loop to the west, emerging at the edge of a wide valley. At its far end lay the Snake River, the waterway hidden somewhere behind a barrier of cottonwood trees that grew thick along its course. McKay and the others would be following that river. Kit Carson did not see them, but he did spy the small smudge upon the valley's floor, moving toward that unseen river.

"Thar you red devils are," he said to himself, relief and satisfaction in his voice at the same time. "I'm not too late." He turned his horse toward the valley and worked his way off the rimrock. As trees gave way to grass, the trapper lost sight of the Indians. That was just as well. If he could not see them, they couldn't see him. Laying the ends of his reins sharply across the rump of his horse, he leaned low in the saddle and raced across the valley floor, aiming at a place along the unseen river forward of where the band of Indians seemed to be heading.

He made the passage without another glimpse of the Blackfeet. Once within the cottonwoods, Kit drew up at the banks of the Snake River and gave his horse a well-deserved drink, all the time on the look out for the war party.

135

"Let's go," he whispered, pulling the horse's head from the water and clucking softly. Somewhere up ahead he would find McKay. The only question now was where and how far. The leader of the Oregon-bound immigrants would have almost certainly kept to the open ground; not to the trees, where travel was difficult if not impossible for a caravan of wagons. Especially since McKay still did not know he was being trailed by a band of murdering Blackfeet.

Kit left cover and for a while followed the ribbon of trees, keeping near them in case he had to duck quickly out of sight. But in his effort to circle ahead of the Blackfeet, he had lost McKay's trail. Now he began searching open ground to pick it up again, all the while keeping an eye on his back trail, knowing that not far behind the Blackfeet were moving up on him.

The job of scouting out the trail took him far from the river, crossing the valley toward the east. Finally, Kit cut the wagon ruts. Among them he discovered many older tracks, as if McKay and others had frequently used this trail to Oregon. It was becoming a regular highway, he mused. More and more folks were moving into this land. One day it would be as crowded as a city, but he judged that time was still far off. At least another two or three hundred years before this wide-open country would be completely civilized and filled up—if it ever happened at all.

He had to hurry now—all at once the hairs at the back of his neck began to tingle and rise. Although he never understood why it happened, he knew that when it did it was time to dive for cover!

Kit swiveled about in his saddle. About a mile off a string of Blackfeet warriors suddenly crested a hill.

They'd spied him about the same time he had caught sight of them. For a moment neither trapper nor Indians moved; then with a sudden rush the war party charged down the hill. Kit yanked his horse around and buried his heels. The weary animal gave a good start, leaping instantly into a full gallop. There was no place to run to, so Kit just pointed the animal's nose in the direction that the wagon tracks lay and, whipping the long ends of his reins, urged her onto greater speed.

Although he had a long head start on these killers, Kit knew he could never hold the lead. He had ridden his horse hard for almost a full day already; the animal was all done in and needed rest. But Kit pushed the mare even harder now, and they flew across the stiff buffalo grass. His sharp blue eyes were in constant motion, casting about for a place to take cover: an outcropping of rock, a defensible ravine, even a decent stand of trees! But the river was too far away to reach in time, and even if he could reach it, and the tall cottonwood trees that marched alongside it, he knew the notion of making a stand was not only nonsense, but plain suicide. He was one man alone against more than two dozen fierce warriors. He had but a single rifle and two pistols, and even if he could reload and fire them faster than most men, he could never overcome such odds!

He had only one chance, and that was to shake these murderers off his trail. But how? Kit glanced over his shoulder again. The Blackfeet were closer. His horse was flagging. He lashed the ends of his reins relentlessly, demanding of the mare everything she had to give. She stumbled, then recovered.

There was nothing ahead but wide-open ground, while behind him certain death was slowly closing in on him. He frowned into the onrush of wind. It appeared the only way he was going to shake these red varmints was if the earth were to open and swallow him up—and he didn't think that very likely.

The landscape flew past and gradually, over the next ten minutes, the Blackfeet gained ground on him.

There was grass and more grass, with a few scattered outcroppings of rocks here and there, and some solitary trees looking lost in this sea of grass. It looked as if his scalp was certain to end up on some buck's lodge pole if he didn't think of something fast. He felt the horse losing steam. Her gait had become uneven, and twice more she nearly stumbled. The Blackfeet were less than a quarter mile off now and closing fast.

Nowhere to hide; nowhere to flee. In spite of the futility of it, Kit had no other choice now but to make the stand that he had hoped he would not have to. Turning the mare's head to the north, Kit angled for a small outcropping of rock surrounded by half-a-dozen tall, wind-battered pine trees. Like lonely sentinels on the wide empty plains, they stood there as if beckoning him to flee to what little protection they could offer.

"This child is a'gonna take a passel of them murdering redskins with him when he goes down," Kit declared as he leaped from the exhausted mare and stripped off his saddlebags where he carried extra powder, caps, and balls. Like a mouse with a cat on its tail, he scurried in among the rocks.

The outcropping was of granite, all sharp-angled

spires looking like teeth sticking up out of the ground. They only rose a dozen or so feet above the surrounding prairie grass, but that extra elevation gave Kit a slight advantage over the men on horseback, now only five hundred yards off. He laid his pistols out and hunkered behind a shoulder of rock, placing bullet bag, patches, powder horn, and capper in easy reach. He removed the rifle stick and placed it within easy reach too.

He worked himself into a little hollow where he was protected from all sides, not that it would matter much once he was surrounded and his shooting-ware empty. He unlimbered his tomahawk and butcher knife and set them near at hand. When the end came, when he finally went down beneath their overwhelming numbers, it would be with these hand-to-hand weapons that he would be fighting his last.

Kit slid his rifle through a gap in the rock, snugged it tight into his shoulder, and thumbed back its hammer. As he watched them coming beyond the sights of the long, octagonal barrel, he thought of Reverend William Pritchard back at the Snake village. He regretted he would not be able to complete his mission of guiding Pritchard to his friends. At the very least, he hoped this standoff would in some way save McKay and his party from these Blackfeet. If only he could cut down their numbers enough to send them packing on home and leave the travelers alone.

The nearest rider was coming into range now, and Kit could not afford to miss his shot. Every bullet had to count if he hoped to bloody their noses bad enough to stop them here and now. His finger curled around the trigger. He caught his breath, steadied the front sight upon the breast of one of the Blackfeet, elevated the muzzle just enough to compensate for the bullet's trajectory, and pulled the trigger.

The boom of the heavy buffalo rifle rolled out across the prairie. Three hundred yards away, the Indian let out a yelp and flipped off the back of his horse, instantly disappearing beneath the pounding hooves of the horses behind him. Kit didn't wait to see the results of the shot. His hands raced, spilling powder down the barrel, thumbing a patched ball into the muzzle, and ramming it down hard with the rifle stick. He snapped a fresh cap onto the nipple, hauled back the hammer, and picked out his next target. Now no more than 150 yards out, the riders had begun to move apart. Kit's second bullet shattered the shoulder of an incoming rider, slugging him to the ground like a giant fist.

Then they were in close, riding around the rocks, yelping and drawing back on their bowstrings. Kit ducked. A volley of arrows clattered against the stone all around him. He managed to get the rifle loaded for a third time, and another warrior careened off his horse beyond the cloud of gray gun smoke. Then the Blackfeet were leaping from their horses and dashing for the rocks.

Kit grabbed up his pistols and parted the forehead of the first man to clamber over the rocks. As he caved backwards, another warrior materialized out the corner of Kit's eye. Whirling around, Kit shot a hole through the man's neck, and he lurched backward and out of sight. Kit grabbed up his rifle and smashed the curved, iron butt plate into the scowling mouth of the next face he saw. It disappeared behind a gush of crimson.

Kit's eyes were in constant motion, trying to watch everywhere at once. He had a brief reprieve as the warriors lurked just out of sight, and snatched up a pistol and began to reload it. But just then a wild cry reached him from behind. Instantly he threw himself to one side. A feathered war lance stabbed down, clipping his shirtsleeve. Kit grabbed the shaft of the spear in one hand, his tomahawk in the other, and wheeling around, buried the broad edge of the ax in the Blackfoot's naked chest. Shock and surprise widened the man's eyes, and he stood a moment staring down at the hunk of iron sticking out of his chest. Then he toppled to the ground. Kit wrenched the spear from the man's hands, and as if instinctively knowing where the next attack would come from, he thrust it out.

But the Indian was just as fast. He leaped aside as the spear's point sliced harmlessly through the empty air. Like a jackrabbit the Blackfoot had jumped over the edge of rock brandishing a tomahawk. Kit tried again with the spear. The tomahawk streaked down. Kit reversed his motion and threw the shaft up in front of himself. The ax sliced it in half. There was some movement to his left, a second warrior scrambling over the rocks toward him.

The end was drawing near now for the mountain man as the tomahawk swiped this way and that with the speed of a striking rattlesnake. Distantly, Kit wondered why there were not more men swarming over the rocks than just these two. There should be a dozen by now. But he had no time to ponder that. He barely managed to dodge the swiping tom-

141

ahawk as he backed down the rocky path. Then his heel caught a spur of rock and he stumbled backwards. He tried to stop himself from falling, but his head smacked into a point of rock and the world went momentarily out of focus. When it came back again a second later, the warrior with the tomahawk was standing over him, poised for the final blow. . . .

Thomas McKay frowned at the cart lying on one side like a badly listing boat. The cart belonged to Marcus Whitman and had begun life, and the long journey to Oregon, as a wagon. But en route it had been converted to two-wheel service by the removal of the rear wheels, supposedly to make traveling the narrow trails across the Blue Mountains more navigable. What it did in reality was make the cart a fragile thing that had given them trouble ever since leaving Fort Hall.

Now it sat upon the grass with one wheel shattered and the other badly warped.

"I have a spare, Marcus," his friend and traveling companion, Henry Spalding, offered.

"Thank you, Henry. I am sorry to be such a burden." Whitman stared at the shattered wheel, shaking his head.

McKay gave the order for some of his men to lend a hand. Together they lifted the cart upright and stacked flat stones beneath it to keep it level. Next, Whitman and Spalding crawled under the Spaldings' wagon and began untying the spare wheel stored there.

McKay and his partner, John McLeod, watched the progress from a little way away, discussing the delays. The two traders were anxious to get to Fort

Walla Walla, and had not counted on such slow travel when they'd made the offer to guide these missionaries to Oregon.

Petey Pauly wandered on over, rifle slung over his shoulder, combing bits of food from his long, scraggly beard. Petey was a gaunt beanpole of a man and a loner of the first order. He had just spent three years trapping the Yellow Stone region by himself, and had joined McKay's party because Oregon sounded like a place that was still wide open. Not like these Rocky Mountains that, to Petey's way of thinking, were becoming a mite too crowded for his liking.

"That thar doctor spends more time fixing that wagon than he do riding on it. Say, when do ye coons figure on raising Walla Walla?" Petey glanced at his old rifle and added, "Betsy here says she's plum anxious to be outta of these mountains and see some of that green Oreegon country we've heard tell of. If we like what we see, me and Betsy are gonna stake us a claim to some of it."

McKay glanced at Petey's battered flintlock rifle and said, "You tell Betsy we will arrive when we arrive, Mr. Pauly, and not a day before."

Petey frowned and affectionately patted Betsy's butt. "Hear that, old gal?"

McLeod glanced around warily, then said, "Where is that bear of yours, Mr. Pauly? I get nervous when I don't know when he'll show up next."

"Ebenezer is about somewhar," Petey said confidently. "He fights shy of crowds, ye know."

"Hmm. Somewhere far away, I hope," McLeod replied, scanning the open countryside. No one had yet become comfortable with Petey's traveling companion, a huge grizzly bear that Petey had raised from a cub.

A faint boom reached them from far away. At first McKay thought it to be distant thunder—but then it didn't sound exactly right for that.

McLeod narrowed his eyes toward the east. "That sounded like a rifle to me," he said, giving McKay a questioning look.

"Dang right it was a rifle, hoss!" Petey declared. "These ears of mine can hear a twig snap at a hunder paces and a Blackfoot's breath when he's still a march away. That was a rifle shot sure as if I pulled the trigger myself."

A second boom rolled out of the distance.

Petey's expression took on a suddenly suspicious look.

"What is it?" McKay asked him.

Petey shot them a quick glance. "Call me loco if ye want, hoss, but I swear I've heard that rifle a'fore."

"White man?"

"He war the last time I seen the coon!" Petey dashed for his horse and leaped into the saddle.

McKay glanced at McLeod. They both looked at Petey as the loner kicked his horse into motion and charged out of there.

"To your horses, boys!" McLeod ordered.

Chapter Thirteen

"Well, well, young man, you are looking quite alert now. Good color too."

Climb-to-the-Top peered up from the sleeping pallet where he lay, his mother sitting at his side, preparing to help him eat. Green Hummingbird translated William Pritchard's words as the preacher/surgeon bent over him and pressed a hand to the boy's head.

"No fever yet. Very good." It was still early, and a fever and infection could erupt at almost any time. Pritchard studied the lad's pupils and nodded. "Very good indeed." Glancing at the mother, he added, "See that he drinks lots of water." Turning back to the boy, he said, "The leg hurt?"

Getting the words from Green Hummingbird, Climb-to-the-Top looked back at Pritchard and emphatically shook his head, his face stern and unflinching.

Pritchard laughed. "I know that is a lie. The laudanum wore off hours ago. But I admire your grit, son!" He glanced at Green Hummingbird. "You need not translate that.

"I will stop by in the morning to see how you are getting along, Mr. Climb-to-the-Top." He and Green Hummingbird left the tipi. The young woman moved with some discomfort, with fingers interlocked beneath her swelled belly as if to give it extra support.

"Are you all right, Green Hummingbird?"

She nodded.

"When are you due?"

"Due?"

At her blank look, he pointed and said, "The baby inside you, when is he to be born? Soon?"

A grin suddenly spread her dusky cheeks, and her brown eyes glistened in the afternoon sunlight. "Yes. Very soon."

He smiled. "I wish I could stay, to be here to greet him . . . or her, as the case may be."

"You cannot stay?" There was a note of concern in her voice.

"I must be leaving soon. I have to go to Oregon—with my friends."

"Soon? How soon?"

"Tomorrow—or the day after at the very least. It all depends on how well Climb-to-the-Top is doing." He thought he saw her frown, but she had glanced away from him too quickly.

As they strolled away from Climb-to-the-Top's tipi, Pritchard heard his name called—at least he thought it was his name. *Pris-shurd?*

They stopped and looked around. Laughing

Water Woman was standing in the doorway of her lodge. Upon catching their eye, the old woman waved an arm.

"I wonder what she wants."

Green Hummingbird shrugged. "I do not know."

They walked over, and the matriarch motioned for them to come inside. As Pritchard ducked through the door, Laughing Water Woman lowered herself to a buffalo-skin rug, tilted her head up toward him, and opened her mouth.

Standing there, staring down into the yawning gap, Pritchard was momentarily dumbfounded.

The old woman jabbed a finger at her mouth.

"You want me to look at the tooth?"

The woman spoke. Green Hummingbird said, "Grandmother watched you stop the flow of blood and close the skin. It is a big medicine that you do. She says that Elijah is indeed a great and powerful medicine man."

Pritchard winced. He had almost forgotten the fib he had told these people. Suddenly his conscience was pricked and he wanted to straighten the matter out, but wondered if it would be wise to do so just then.

"She say she will let medicine man Elijah look in her mouth now."

His confession would have to wait, he decided, taking the old woman's head gently into his hands and turning it toward the light. He peered at the teeth, which were badly worn down from years of eating coarse food. A pair of molars on one side of the jaw were in a horrible condition. One was cracked clear down to the puffy swollen gums. Both had severe rot in them. The inflamed tissue that surrounded the teeth was painful just to look at, and from beneath the two bad teeth, and the adjacent molars, yellow, viscous pus seeped into her mouth. There were pouches of the "yellow poison" all along the gum.

"A very bad infection here," he said, frowning. The malodorous stench of diseased flesh from her mouth assaulted Pritchard's nose with each breath she took. He stood back and shook his head. "Tell Laughing Water Woman that I will try to help her if she wishes me to. Tell her there is much poison in her mouth and that I will have to remove at least two of her teeth."

Green Hummingbird translated.

The old woman nodded her head.

Green Hummingbird said, "She will permit you to make your medicine."

"Very well. I shall need my instruments."

He left to get his leather medical bag. By the time he returned, word of his next healing session had already drawn a crowd of curious women and men to the tipi. Among those gathered there, Pritchard recognized the old man with long gray hair who earlier had tried to stop him from treating Climb-to-the-Top. Green Hummingbird was standing with this old man, apparently explaining something to him. But when Pritchard entered the tipi, she was once again at his side.

After laying out his instruments, Pritchard got to work at once. It was a simple matter to remove the rotting teeth. After cleaning the area to better see what he was doing, Pritchard grabbed the cracked molar in the jaws of a heavy pair of extraction pliers. With a twist and tug, the tooth cracked apart and came out in three pieces. Immediately pus shot from the wound as if under great pressure. He swabbed it out, marveling at the old woman's command of the pain, which must have been tremendous. Laughing Water Woman hardly flinched. He removed the second tooth, with much the same results. When he finished, both holes in the woman's jaw were freely flowing pus mixed with blood. Pritchard encouraged the flow, using a wooden probe to gently prod the gums, milking the pus from them.

He finished with a bit of cotton wool, soaked in alcohol and pressed gently into the gaps. This caused her more distress than the actual removal of the teeth. But he saw by the new life in her eyes that already the suffering she had endured for so many weeks was subsiding. Not surprising, considering that the extraction had relieved so much internal pressure. And now that the "yellow poison" was draining freely, he suspected marked improvement would follow swiftly.

He showed Laughing Water Woman the fragments of the teeth he had removed. "These will cause you no further difficulty, ma'am."

She peered at them, expressionless.

"In a few weeks you will hardly miss them at all," he assured her.

"Ninnimbe," was all the old woman managed to mumble, shaking her head.

Pritchard gave her a questioning look. But she said nothing more. He collected his instruments, wiping them with a piece of wet cloth as he returned them to his leather bag. When he finished, he said he'd return later to look in on her. He asked Green

Hummingbird about the herbs and poultices her people used to fight infections. She told him what should be used, and he suggested that they be employed now, to aid the healing process.

Afternoon shadows were lengthening across the village when he stepped outside again. Several of the curious onlookers poked their heads in the doorway. Upon the old woman's invitation, four women stepped inside.

He spied Green Hummingbird hurrying toward her tipi. The ordeal had worn her out; a pregnancy as late-term as hers appeared to be was certainly a wearisome thing, even to these hardy people. Pritchard had to admire their capacity to endure pain. Laughing Water Woman had hardly uttered a whimper at what must have been a most agonizing trial to her.

He returned to the empty tipi he had been staying in, and stretched out upon the skin rug. He was tired. Thinking back over the day, he was amazed at all that had happened, that it was only this morning when he was packing his mules and declaring his resolve to leave. He gave a wry smile and a short laugh. "How easily the circumstances of life do intrude in the plans of men!"

Even though he had not left the village to search for his friends as he had intended to, William Pritchard felt strangely at peace with himself here. All in all, it had been a good day.

He sat up to watch village life beyond the doorway of the tipi. A dog romped past, then two little boys chasing him. Women carrying bundles and baskets and babies strolled by in twos and threes. There were low conversations drifting in through the skins of the tipi from several quarters. Most of the men, he noted, were older, the younger ones being away at the war with the Blackfeet. That thought disturbed Pritchard, and he did not know why it should. Why should he care about these Shoshoni? A needling worry began worming its way into his brain. Green Hummingbird was soon to give birth, and her husband Swift Running Antelope was away at war. What if he should not return? In Pritchard's brief stay with these people, Green Hummingbird and Swift Running Antelope had become especially important to him.

In the midst of fretting over Swift Running Antelope's safety, Pritchard failed to notice the sudden rise in activity outside. It was only when two women carrying bundles under their arms hurried past and ducked quickly into Green Hummingbird's tipi that he realized something was happening. He stepped outside as a third woman disappeared behind the door flap of the tipi. Many of the women who sat in front of their tipis seemed to be listening for some sound.

Pritchard started for Green Hummingbird's tipi.

A hand reached out and caught him by the arm. When he turned, that same old man was there, peering at him. He was surprised at the strength in the man's bony fingers. He tried to break free of the grip. The old man only squeezed tighter and gave a firm shake of his head. No words passed between the two of them, yet Pritchard understood clearly what the old man was trying to tell him. This was something that he could not be a part of—something that was not in the realm of men, but for the women only.

Pritchard stopped struggling and simply nodded his head. The old man gave the briefest of smiles and released him.

All Pritchard could do was wait, like the rest of them.

Gazing up into the burning eyes of certain death, Kit Carson knew he had reached his end. Too stunned to fight, overwhelmed and weaponless, he could do nothing but stare as the tomahawk swept down. . . .

Then something flickered past him. He'd caught only a glimpse of it out of the corner of his eye. The Indian jerked backward, a wide, startled look suddenly upon his face as an arrow out of nowhere sunk deep into his chest.

Another arrow whistled in, and the second Blackfoot staggered back, groping at the shaft that had ripped through his neck.

Still reeling from the shock of the fall and blow to his head, and now from the shock of this sudden reversal of fortune, Kit only distantly became aware of the pounding of hooves and the mingling of war cries. Pulling himself up and then to his knees, he peered past a spire of rock. Charging in among the Blackfeet was Hunting Wolf and his band of Shoshoni warriors. Kit understood now why only two of the Blackfeet had come for him. The others had apparently seen the Shoshonis approaching and had turned to repel the attack.

The two forces collided, and the shrill of the battle rang across the open land. After the first few volleys, bows and arrows gave way to knives and tomahawks as the Shoshonis leaped off their horses.

Kit shook off his grogginess, grabbed up his knife, and yanked his tomahawk from the breast of the lifeless Indian crumpled nearby. Yelling out the war cry of a Rocky Mountain Boy, he leaped over the craggy rampart and plunged into the thick of the battle.

Moving in among the Blackfeet, Kit deflected a driving war lance and came in low and swiftly with his knife. He turned to parry a slashing tomahawk, and his own tomahawk took a deep bite out of the man's shoulder, sending him howling to the ground.

Kit spied Hunting Wolf nearby, lashing out like a demon, raining deathblows upon these murderers of his family.

In the heat of battle it was difficult to separate Shoshoni from Blackfoot. Kit worked his way alongside Calling Elk, taking his cue from the stout medicine man. They exchanged glances, and Kit gave Calling Elk a fleeting grin.

"Right pleased that you boys showed up when you did." He wheeled about to face a new challenge and said over his shoulder, "This child owes you his skin."

Calling Elk dispatched the warrior he'd been fighting and replied, "Now we have settled what is owed for saving Buffalo Pony."

Kit never expected repayment for a good deed, and he knew that neither did Reverend Pritchard. But this was no time to dispute the medicine man's statement.

Kit lost sight of Calling Elk as a band of howling Blackfeet closed in on them. The next few minutes the two armies fought to a standoff. But the Shoshonis clearly outnumbered the Blackfeet, with many among them who Kit did not recognize as being with the original party.

The Blackfeet understood their hopeless position, and began to give ground. Then a call for retreat sounded, and those left standing ran for their horses, leaping upon their animals and fleeing before the scorn of the Shoshonis, who followed afoot a few paces before turning back to see to their losses.

Kit stared at the destruction all around him as he heaved in gulps of air and slowly straightened out of his fighting crouch. The Shoshonis began to tend to their wounded while a small band of warriors swarmed over the downed Blackfeet, taking scalps and killing those who still breathed.

Kit watched the escaping Blackfeet racing across the tawny grass, growing smaller in the distance as they fled the bloody battleground.

Less than ten of Blackfeet had escaped, and there was some talk about pursuit from a knot of men nearby, but their words were cut off by the sudden staccato of gunfire. Kit's head snapped back around, and at the same time half the fleeing Blackfeet tumbled from their horses, while the few remaining veered off toward the river. In a moment a company of men on horseback pounded up over a small rise of land and into view. They were too far off for Kit to identify, but he was certain it was McKay and his men. Who else could it have been? The men drew up suddenly when they spied the Shoshonis. Kit was about to flag them over when he saw Hunting Wolf with two other men kneeling upon the ground near one of the fallen men.

It was Calling Elk!

Kit hurried over just as the young warrior with

the scar down his cheek dropped to his knees besides the older man. Weakly, Calling Elk removed a pouch from around his neck and handed it to the younger man. Except for the scar, the two faces were so much alike that they could only be father and son. The older man said something so low Kit could not hear. But his son did, and nodding, he squeezed his father's hand. Then Calling Elk closed his eyes and breathed his last.

Kit grimaced as he walked a little distance apart from them and waved an arm for McKay and the others to come on in. Slowly, cautiously, the white men approached. Some of the Shoshonis readied their weapons, but Kit assured Hunting Wolf that these men were his friends.

Chapter Fourteen

Reverend William Pritchard nervously paced up and down the village, his hands clasped tightly behind his back, an ear tuned toward the tipi where hours before the ordeal had begun.

"You'd think I was the husband!" he declared to himself at one point.

As dusk drew its dark blanket over the village and the leaping lights of half a dozen fires began to dance wildly among the tipis, he strolled toward Laughing Water Woman's lodge, thinking to check up on his latest patient. But he stopped before announcing himself at the door. Without his translator at his side he was helpless.

He glanced across the way at the tipi where a woman carrying a gourd of water was at this moment entering. In only one day he had grown quite fond of that young girl; her anxious smile, her willingness to stay near his side to help him understand her people. He wished he could be at her side, to help where he could. But in this village, in this culture, that was not to be.

It occurred to Pritchard that he could learn their language if he tried. Mr. Carson spoke it well enough, and certainly if Running Antelope and Green Hummingbird could learn English, he could learn Shoshoni. . . .

Pritchard nipped that line of thinking in the bud. He was not staying here, after all! He was going on to Oregon, where the Indians spoke an entirely different tongue!

He walked down to the stream for a drink of water. Afterward, he stood and surveyed the small valley in the gathering dusk. Overhead, nighthawks had begun their frantic feeding, diving and swooping for insects, sometimes so near to him that Pritchard could hear the whoosh of their wings mere inches from his head. Up the valley, the night guards built a small fire by the horse corral. In the village, many of the tipis glowed like covered lamps from the cook fires flickering inside them.

The stories he had heard about the Shoshoni had been anything but complimentary, yet here, with this group at least, he had discovered a friendly people who showed much industry and compassion.

He returned to the village, and was immediately summoned over to one of the fires where Laughing Water Woman was seated along with six others. She appeared still in much pain, but there was a fresh vitality in her face that had been missing before. Her old eyes glistened in the firelight as she smiled at him and indicated that he should sit with them.

Among them was the old, gray-haired man. He handed Pritchard a woven mat and a bowl made from a hollowed piece of wood, and indicated the food.

Dinner was sliced elk, which had been wrapped in the broad leaves of some local plant and baked among hot stones. There was bread of some unknown origin too—not made of ground wheat as he was used to eating, but tasty nonetheless. And finally, a soup of vegetable and meat. He'd earlier observed the curious manner in which they cooked soups and stews. It was done in a leather bag, which looked suspiciously like the stomach of some large animal, suspended by a tripod. The women would heat round river rocks in a fire, then plop them sizzling-hot into the bag, slowly bringing the liquid to nearly a boil.

He ate without speaking as he listened to their conversation, not understanding a word of it. But the occasional laugh, a groan followed by a look of disgust or pleasure, this was a universal tongue that he readily understood. Except for the lack of civilized utensils, and a language that rang foreign in his ears, this gathering of people was like any other family group he had ever known. Strangely, he felt at ease among them. In spite of differences as wide as the Atlantic, the similarities were startling!

The sudden squall of a baby brought an instant halt to their talk. Indeed, it seemed to Pritchard that the whole village had come to an abrupt stop to listen with heads bent toward the tipi where Green Hummingbird had exiled herself earlier that day. As if to confirm their suspicions, and to announce its arrival to the world, the baby cried out again.

The villagers resumed their lives, and the people sitting with Pritchard began to laugh and chat. Someone reached over and gave the old man an affectionate pat on the shoulder. He gave a missing-tooth grin in return, and Pritchard could not help but grin like a fool with him and the rest of them.

A little while later, a woman emerged and spread the news. Pritchard was dying to learn if it was a boy or a girl. He stood with some of the tribe members near the door, hoping as they were to catch a glimpse. Finally, the door flap opened and Green Hummingbird emerged, holding a little bundle wrapped in soft rabbit skin. Everyone wanted a peek. Pritchard managed to work his way near to her.

"Congratulations. Is it a boy or a girl?"

She glanced around the faces until she found his. "Him is a little man," she said. Her face beamed with pride and delight.

After a while several of the elders, including the old man, entered the tipi with Green Hummingbird and shut the door. An hour or so later they emerged from the lodge and sat around a fire, smoking a pipe of tobacco and passing it between then as they discussed something in earnest. Occasionally, one of the men would raise his eyes and stare at Pritchard. He would have given a hundred dollars to know what they were discussing. But it was not for him to know—at least not yet.

Green Hummingbird remained in her tipi the rest of the evening, and Pritchard finally retired to his borrowed lodge and went to sleep.

The next morning Green Hummingbird brought him breakfast. She had her new baby securely bound in a cradleboard, a contraption not unlike the one in which Pritchard had discovered Buffalo Pony in that grove of trees. Green Hummingbird seemed completely unaffected by the ordeal of the birth, and was up and about her daily routine as if nothing out of the ordinary had occurred. How unlike the women of his acquaintance. Edith, his dear, departed, excitable wife, when she had given birth to their son, spent most of two weeks in bed recovering.

"How are you feeling?" he asked.

"Feel?"

He grinned. "You appear quite well. The birth, it was easy?"

She tried to fathom the nature of his question. Finally grasping it, Green Hummingbird laughed and said, "Little man, him fight, but come anyway."

He laughed with her, and at the simple summation of the matter. "May I hold him?"

She passed the cradleboard across to him. Pritchard made baby sounds to entertain the little fellow, even though the newborn was not yet capable of appreciating his efforts. The baby was barely able to keep his eyes open. At least the newborn was securely bundled in the cradleboard, so Pritchard had no fear of another warm shower.

"What have you named him?"

"Grandfather give boy name."

"Oh, is that how it is done amongst your people?"

"Yes."

"Hmm. And what name did your grandfather give him?"

She smiled, then cautiously looked around the tipi and lowered her voice. "Him call name Elijah, because someday him be a great medicine man like him grandfather, like him father, like Pritchard."

Pritchard frowned. This had gone on too long. He asked her to sit down for he had something to tell her. "You know," he started slowly, thoughtfully, looking at the baby in his arms because he was too ashamed to look directly at her. "I have a confession to make, Green Hummingbird. I am afraid that I have been less than completely truthful to you and your people." At her blank stare he clarified his statement. "I did not speak true words. You see, I was afraid your people would not let me help Climb-to-the-Top, so I . . . I sort of told a little lie."

She blinked, listening intently.

He grimaced. "My people don't really call me by that name, you see. I only said that so that the old man—your grandfather—would not stop me from helping the boy. Not that it is a bad name," he added quickly. "It is a very good name indeed. It was the name of a great medicine man who lived long ago. He was a man who found favor with God and did wonderful things. He raised people from the dead and called fire out of the skies, and in doing so defeated many of his enemies. So you see, it is a very worthy name for a future medicine man. Only, it is not my name."

"You are not a great medicine man?"

Pritchard managed a grin. "Well, I am a medicine man, that is true. But 'great'? I suppose that is debatable."

"You stopped the flow of blood, and closed the skin with your magic thread. And you stopped the yellow poison from stealing away Grandmother's spirit."

"It was science, my dear child, not magic."

"Sci-ence?" She tried the word out a few times,

161

and seemed to like the sound of it. "Then this is powerful medicine, this sci-ence? Yes?"

Pritchard smiled thinly and said, "Oh, some men think so—some believe so fervently in the power of science that they even worship it as a faith. I prefer to think of science as . . . as merely being *useful*."

She considered his confession a moment. "You spoke the name of the long-ago medicine man so that you might help the boy."

"Yes I did, but an end does not justify the means. A lie is a lie, and it was wrong of me to speak it. But Elijah is a very good name for your son."

She looked suddenly concerned and hushed him, putting a finger to her mouth while quickly glancing about.

"What is it?" he asked, casting a furtive glance over his shoulder.

"You must not speak his name loud."

"Whose?"

She nodded at the baby.

"But why?"

"Ninnimbe might hear and learn it."

"Ninnimbe? *Ninnimbe?* Who is this Ninnimbe whom I have heard much of since coming to your village?"

"The Ninnimbe were the little people who lived long ago and made the rock pictures. No one could see them and their arrows were poison. Long ago one of our people saw a Ninnimbe, but now they are all dead. All but one. He still lives. We call him Ninnimbe too. Some say he is a little boy, some say old man. He has big red nose and lives hidden in mountains, coming down with his poison arrows to hurt the people. If he learns a name, he might hurt that person, or kill him with arrows that cannot be seen. Ninnimbe makes mischief and trouble for the People. He makes sickness. He makes horses lame. He brings sadness to the People. His poison arrow hit Grandmother, and Climb-to-the-Top. No Shoshoni will make a journey if they think Ninnimbe is nearby. At night, sometimes, you hear him moving through the village."

Peering into her wide, worried eyes, Pritchard almost smiled. But he didn't. He had the urge to give her a daughterly hug. He didn't do that either. In spite of how he might view Ninnimbe, this was a very real fear to her and her people. He thought a moment about what she had told him.

"You know," he began thoughtfully, "I think I understand about Ninnimbe. He not only makes mischief for the Shoshoni, but he makes trouble for all men. The white men know of him too, and we call him by many different names. Some call him Mephistopheles, others Beelzebub. He is sometimes known as the Prince of Darkness, and Lucifer is a common name. But generally, folks refer to him simply as the devil, and he is feared by many. But he need not be feared at all."

Green Hummingbird listened with wide curiosity, and Pritchard was about to preach a short sermon on the matter when a commotion outside interrupted them. Rising from the buffalo rug and handing little Elijah back to her, Pritchard ducked out the door. Approaching the village was a large company of riders, still a long way off.

"What is it?" Green Hummingbird asked, stopping alongside him.

"It appears that the warriors have returned." He

163

was suddenly excited. "Yes, I am sure that is what it is. And there is Mr. Carson with them. And my old friend Henry Spalding! And someone else too." Pritchard hurried with the villagers to meet them.

While the returning warriors were still fifty yards off, he stopped, staring at the string of horses carrying the bodies. His heart crawled up into his throat and he glanced back at Green Hummingbird, who was watching from the village's edge with three other women. He looked again, searching for Swift Running Antelope. At first he didn't see the young man. Then there he was, riding at the rear of the company, leading an animal with a body folded across its back. A wave of relief swept over Pritchard.

"William!" Henry Spalding shouted upon seeing Pritchard.

"Henry! And Mr. Carson! Am I glad to see you!"

Kit, Spalding, and the stranger reined to a stop as the ragtag warriors, with the wounded and dead, passed them by. The third man was Thomas McKay. Kit made the introduction.

From the village came the rising wail of women as they learned the fate of their husbands and sons. Pritchard grimaced. "I take it you found the Indians who murdered Little Chief's family?"

"Found the murderers, all right," Kit said. "And this child almost lost his scalp to them, but Hunting Wolf showed up just in time to rout the red devils. A few seconds later and I'd have gone under."

"It was a violent fight," Spalding said, shaking his head. "The others and I arrived just as the Blackfeet were on the run. Mr. McKay and his boys mostly finished the job that Kit and these Indians began." He frowned heavily. "There was much violence and bloodshed."

As Swift Running Antelope rode past, Pritchard stopped him. "I am pleased to see that you are unharmed."

The young warrior nodded his head, sadness etched deep in the bronze skin of his face. Pritchard glanced at the body slung across the pony. "That is Calling Elk," the reverend said.

Swift Running Antelope said, "He died as a Shoshoni should die. Fighting his enemy."

"Calling Elk was your father, wasn't he?"

Swift Running Antelope nodded again.

"I am sorry. I am truly sorry." Then Pritchard remembered the good news. He gave a little small grin and said, "Oh, by the way, congratulations."

The warrior raised a questioning eyebrow. A curious look came to his stern face.

"You are now a father yourself. You have a son."

His eyes widened. "Green Hummingbird?"

"She is just fine. She waits for you by your tipi."

"Whal, you're looking fit as a fiddle, Little Chief . . . err, I mean Buffalo Pony," Kit Carson declared, rocking the baby in his arms. "Don't look like that buffalo milk hurt you one bit."

"Don't say his name too loudly," Pritchard warned.

"Why is that?"

"Ninnimbe might hear."

Kit stared at him, wondering if he was pulling his leg, but if he was, the preacher never cracked a smile.

"They believe it to bring bad luck," he explained.

"I see." Kit grinned as he handed the baby back to the woman. "Ninnimbe, huh? Looks to me like you have done right well for yourself with these people, Reverend. And you not speaking even a word of thar tongue."

"They are an easy people to get to know, and Green Hummingbird was a devoted translator, though I fear I greatly strained her limited vocabulary."

Henry Spalding said, "We need to leave soon." He glanced at Thomas McKay, standing by his side, and added, "Mr. McKay has been quite patient with us so far, but he grows impatient with the delays we have caused him."

McKay told him to think nothing of it.

"I'll help you load up those mules," Kit offered.

With a certain reluctance, Pritchard went about the task of tying all his belongings onto the *aparejo* packsaddles. After the mules were packed and Pritchard's horse saddled, Kit said his farewell to Chief Hunting Wolf.

Swift Running Antelope and Green Hummingbird . . . and Elijah . . . came to say good-bye to Pritchard. Kit could see there was real affection on the couple's faces. The preacher had made friends here during his short stay, and he seemed to be having a hard time with the parting. With a lump in his throat, Pritchard admonished them both to look out for little Elijah.

He turned to his horse and stuck a foot in the stirrup. Laughing Water Woman emerged from her tipi, carrying a parfleche in her withered old hands. Wordlessly, she gave the leather pouch to him, then pointed at her jaw, smiled, and nodded her head.

"You are looking much better this morning," he

said, peeking inside the leather pouch. It was filled with pemmican. Through Green Hummingbird, he gave her a deeply felt thank-you. Once again he attempted to mount his horse, but just then he spied Climb-to-the-Top, hobbling on one leg at his father's side, coming toward him. Shyly, the boy handed him a well-used rawhide ball—the very same ball Pritchard had pitched to him before the accident.

"Thank you," he said, unable to speak further as his Adam's apple bobbed up and down a couple times. He blinked hard and stared at the ball, rubbing his thumb over the coarse seams before putting it in his pocket.

Pritchard swung up onto his saddle. Kit and McKay started out of the village, but the preacher remained a moment longer, looking around the place. With a heavy heart, he raised a hand in parting to the friends. Wearing a frown, he started away from there.

He paused outside the village to look back. Then turned away and urged his horse ahead, to catch up with his friends. But after a half-dozen strides, he reined to a stop for a second time.

"What is the matter, William?" Spalding inquired upon riding back to his friend's side.

"It is hard to kick against the pricks, Henry."

"What are you talking about?"

Pritchard grimaced. "Ever since arriving here—forcibly, I might add—I have been planning my escape. It was to Oregon I felt called, and to Oregon I stubbornly strove. But now I am not so sure. There is this small voice I keep hearing, and keep trying to shut out."

Henry Spalding looked at him gravely. "And what is it this small voice is telling you to do, William?"

He grimaced. "It is telling me that this is where I am needed. Not Oregon. It is telling me I ought to stay right here."

Kit moved his horse closer and leaned forward. "You don't even know thar language, Reverend."

"I know it's crazy, but I could learn."

"You'll get over it, Reverend," Kit assured him. "Some of these Injuns do grow on a fellow. Shoot, I just went and married me one!"

But Spalding disagreed. "William, if this is where you think you are meant to be, then by all means this is where you should stay."

Pritchard gave his friend a tight smile. "I figured you would understand."

Kit said, "You mean to tell me you are really fixing to stay here, with these Snakes?"

He nodded his head. "They need me and what I can offer. Just as much as those people that Mr. Spalding is going to. Yes, I guess I really am going to stay."

"Whal, reckon you know what's right, Reverend. But it might be a long time before you see another white man."

"It will be all right, Mr. Carson."

Kit glanced at McKay, then Spalding. "Reckon this is where we part. I got me a company of Rocky Mountain Boys to catch up with, and since Reverend Pritchard is staying right here, I figure my job is finished."

"Thank you, Mr. Carson," Pritchard said, extending a hand.

"You're welcome, Reverend. You take care of yourself here. If I'm ever in the area I'll try to look you up."

"Do that, please. I will surely have many letters that you can take with you. And someday I will have to return—at least to replenish my supplies. Perhaps when the time comes, you can guide me."

Kit grinned. "Be happy to, Reverend."

"William," Spalding began, swallowing down a lump, "this is good-bye then, until we meet again."

"And we will. Someday I will complete my trip to Oregon, and when I do, I will look you up."

"Our house will always be open to you."

McKay and Spalding started away. Pritchard stared after them a long while, then looked at Kit. "Well, Mr. Carson, you need to be on your way. You've a lot of miles to cover, and if I were you, I'd take an extra day or two and spend it with that new bride of yours."

Kit grinned. "I just might do that." Then his face took on a more somber cast. "Want me to wait here while you make sure these folks really want you to stay with them?"

Pritchard glanced at the village. Green Hummingbird and Swift Running Antelope were standing, watching. "No, that won't be necessary, Mr. Carson." Then he smiled. "Besides, they must let me stay. I have patients to tend to, and there are at least two babies I wish to see do some growing. Good-bye, Mr. Carson, and Godspeed."

"Godspeed to you, Reverend." Kit turned his horse away, then back. "I'll swing by these parts next year, Reverend, to see how it's going for you."

"I'll look for you."

"R'nd'vou' at Horse Creek again next year. Some of these bucks likely come to trade thar. You might hitch a ride with them."

"I'll remember that."

Kit reined his horse around and rode away from there. He did not look back, but he felt Pritchard's eyes watching him all the way across the valley until the forest closed in around him. He would come back someday to see how the preacher was faring. Someday soon, he promised himself as he angled east and north toward the Yellow Stone country where friends . . . and a wife . . . waited for him.

KIT CARSON

The frontier adventures of a true American legend.

#2: *Ghosts of Lodore*. When Kit finds himself hurtling down the Green River into an impossibly high canyon, his first worry is to find a way out—until he comes face-to-face with a primitive Indian tribe preparing for a battle in which, one way or another, he will have to take sides.

___4325-4 $3.99 US/$4.99 CAN

#1: *The Colonel's Daughter*. Kit Carson's courage and strength as an Indian fighter have earned him respect throughout the West. And when the daughter of a Missouri colonel is kidnapped, Kit is determined to find her—even if he has to risk his life to do it!

___4295-9 $3.99 US/$4.99 CAN

KIT CARSON

REDCOAT RENEGADES
DOUG HAWKINS

When Kit Carson arrives in the rich fur-trapping country of the Flatheads, he finds unexpected enemies waiting for him. A renegade British fur agent has been stirring the local tribes into a war of vengeance against the Americans, including their new captive—Kit. Suddenly it falls to Kit to stop the war before it starts . . . or become the first casualty.

___4368-8 $3.99 US/$4.99 CAN

KIT CARSON

KEELBOAT CARNAGE
DOUG HAWKINS

The untamed frontier is filled with dangers of all kinds—both natural and man-made—dangers that only the bravest can survive. And so far Kit Carson has survived them all. But when he sets out north along the Missouri River he has no idea what lies ahead. He can't know that the Blackfeet are out to turn the river red with blood. And when he hitches a ride on a riverboat, he can't know that keelboat pirates are waiting just around the bend!

___4411-0 $3.99 US/$4.99 CAN

KIT CARSON

COMANCHE RECKONING

DOUG HAWKINS

There is probably no better tracker in the West than the famous Kit Carson. With his legendary ability to read sign, it is said he can track a mouse over smooth rock. So Kit doesn't expect any trouble when he sets out on the trail of a common thief. But he hasn't counted on a fierce blizzard that seems determined to freeze his bones. Or on a band of furious Comanches led by an old enemy of Kit's—an enemy dead set on revenge.

___4453-6 $3.99 US/$4.99 CAN

KIT CARSON

BLOOD RENDEZVOUS
DOUG HAWKINS

The high point of any trapper's year is the summer rendezvous, the annual gathering where mountain men from all over the frontier meet to trade the pelts they risked their lives for. But for Kit Carson, the real danger lies in getting to the rendezvous. He is leading a party of trappers, all of them weighed down with a year's worth of furs. That is enough to make them a tempting target for any killer on the trail—especially when the trail leads through Blackfoot territory.

___4499-4 $3.99 US/$4.99 CAN

Dorchester Publishing Co., Inc.
P.O. Box 6640
Wayne, PA 19087-8640

Please add $1.75 for shipping and handling for the first book and $.50 for each book thereafter. NY, NYC, and PA residents, please add appropriate sales tax. No cash, stamps, or C.O.D.s. All orders shipped within 6 weeks via postal service book rate. Canadian orders require $2.00 extra postage and must be paid in U.S. dollars through a U.S. banking facility.

Name_____
Address_____
City_____State_____Zip_____
I have enclosed $_____ in payment for the checked book(s).
Payment <u>must</u> accompany all orders. ❑ Please send a free catalog.
CHECK OUT OUR WEBSITE! www.dorchesterpub.com